W9-BIK-659

FALCON
WILD

Good Shepherd School
145 Jersey Ave. S.
Golden Valley, MN 55426

FALCON
WILD

~~~

TERRY LYNN JOHNSON

~~~

SCHOLASTIC INC.

For Denis, my heart wild

No part of this publication may be reproduced, stored in a retrieval system, or transmitted in any form or by any means, electronic, mechanical, photocopying, recording, or otherwise, without written permission of the publisher. For information regarding permission, write to Charlesbridge Publishing, Inc., 85 Main Street, Watertown, MA 02472.

ISBN 978-1-338-26116-5

Text copyright © 2017 by Terry Lynn Johnson. Cover illustrations copyright © 2017 by Cliff Nielsen. All rights reserved. Published by Scholastic Inc., 557 Broadway, New York, NY 10012, by arrangement with Charlesbridge Publishing, Inc. SCHOLASTIC and associated logos are trademarks and/or registered trademarks of Scholastic Inc.

The publisher does not have any control over and does not assume any responsibility for author or third-party websites or their content.

12 11 10 9 8 7 6 5 4 3 2   18 19 20 21 22

Printed in the U.S.A.   40

First Scholastic printing, November 2017

Display type set in Canvas 3D Sans Regular by Yellow Design Studio
Text type set in Adobe Caslon Pro by Adobe Systems Incorporated
Designed by Susan Mallory Sherman

ONE

Stark senses my fear and pulls at the jesses around her feet. I stroke her breast feathers to calm us both. Trainers should never show nerves to a bird of prey.

I try to slow my breathing as I listen to Dad introduce lure training—my part of the demo. It's my specialty. His falcon, Gremlin, isn't even hooded and sits patiently on his fist, making me regret my insistence on showing Stark. She's not as seasoned as Gremlin. This is her first school demonstration with me. Surveying the crowd, I can't remember why I thought this would be a good idea.

My favorite lure is hidden in my satchel. It's a weighted, stuffed bit of leather in the shape of a duck at the end of a long string. I've already attached a tidbit of meat with the ties in the center. The lure is ready, and Stark is ready. But for the first time since I started helping with demos, I'm not sure I am ready.

"Is it heavy?" asks a girl on the bench behind where I'm

standing. She's probably my age, since we're doing this demo for an eighth-grade biology class. Her straight blond hair falls in a glossy sheet over her shoulders, nothing like my frizzy auburn hair.

She points to Stark, and the two girls sittin̶ ̶ ̶ ̶ giggle. I realize I'm still staring at her and rush ̶ ̶ ̶

"Gyrfalcons are the largest falcons in North Am̶ And females are bigger than males, so she can get heav̶ Almost the same weight as a bowling ball," I say. "I mean, the small kinds of balls. You know the kind you bowl with when they have all the neon lights going, like it's a party? It actually was my party. We went on my birthday."

From the look on her face, I know I need to stop rambling. But I hear myself reaching to keep her attention. "My neighbor Michelle came bowling with us. She lives a few houses down. We've been friends for ages even though she's three years older than me. She goes to school." *Stop talking. Stop it.* "Maybe you know her, Michelle Miller?"

Before the girl can answer, I feel a shift in the audience as all eyes turn to me. My attention snaps back to Dad.

"My daughter, Karma, is one of the best bird handlers in Montana. She'll show you how fast falcons can fly by swinging a lure for Stark to chase," he says. "Stark is a gyrfalcon, the same family as Gremlin, my peregrine here. Are you ready to meet her?"

I give the girl an apologetic smile, then stand taller and walk to the center of the pit. One of the teachers starts a round of polite clapping. The October sky hangs blue and clear. A brisk northerly picks up speed coming off the mountain range to the west and sweeps across the sagebrush. A perfect day for a flight. I turn on my headset microphone and launch quickly into my speech.

"Here at the education center, we have hawks, falcons, eagles, and owls. We call them all raptors, which is a term for birds of prey. Falcons, like Stark here, have long, thin toes." I point to her gorgeous yellow feet.

"Their beaks are short, with a notch that acts like a tooth. It fits between the neck vertebrae of their prey. Falcons kill prey by breaking their necks. Hawks, however, have strong feet and talons for gripping and puncturing vital organs. That's how *they* kill prey."

As I recite my speech, I walk the perimeter so everyone can see Stark up close. Later they'll have a chance to hold one of the kestrels, our smallest falcons.

"Some raptors' talons can apply four hundred pounds of pressure. Humans can maybe squeeze twenty pounds." I pause for effect before the punch line. "Depends how much you work out."

Scattered laughter makes me smile as I make eye contact with everyone. All the best performers make eye contact. The blond girl doesn't smile back. She talks to her friends behind her hand. My stomach tightens as I wonder if they're talking about me.

I keep my left arm angled to comfortably hold the three-pound falcon and not tire myself. Normally, all my attention is on the bird on my fist, but I can't help sneaking glances at the three girls. Are they impressed with Stark's white plumage? Maybe they wish they owned a falcon. I should have said more about falcons instead of bowling. Why do I always do that? If I'd been more interesting, maybe they would've wanted to visit, which could've led to a friendship—and then to sleepovers with pizza and sharing secrets. All the regular things I imagine friends do.

Stark holds her beak partially open as she shuffles on my gloved hand, and I automatically pinch the jesses between my fingers to keep her from flying off.

"Falconers like to stick with tradition and use old-fashioned words for things," I say. "For example, we call this glove I'm wearing to protect me from the talons a gauntlet."

I point to the other pieces of equipment. "The leather bracelets on Stark's legs are called anklets, and the thinner leather straps that hang down from the anklets are jesses. The legs are the strongest part of the bird."

I reach for Stark's hood, but my attention strays to the girls. The moment the hood is off, Stark's sharp beak sinks into my bare arm just above the glove. I yelp in pain and surprise.

Fighting the same panic that surely courses through Stark's own body, I force myself to calmly gather the jesses between my fingers and go still. The worst thing to do is what I want to do—scream and shake my arm.

I am calm. I am not afraid. I am safety.

Guilt sticks in my throat as she bates, trying to fly away from me. The jesses prevent her from leaving my fist. She hangs upside down, flapping. I wait until she pauses, and then I swing her upright, my jaw clenched. I should've noticed she was unsure of the crowd. I should've paid attention.

The blood is thick and red as it trickles into my gauntlet and down my wrist.

Her wings deliver blows across my face. To avoid them, I straighten my arm and accidentally loosen my fingers, releasing her jesses—something I haven't done since I was seven. Stark rises into the sky with her jesses still attached. If she flies to a tree and they tangle in the branches, I will never forgive myself. I'm supposed to keep her safe, but I've let her down.

Students shriek and point in the air, shoving each other. Dad secures Gremlin to a block and then swings a lure. He whistles to my bird in the sky.

Shamefaced and shocked, I stare at the skin of my forearm, already purpling around the punctures. Now that I don't need to pretend composure for Stark, my hands begin to shake. My knees won't work properly. I gape at the chaos of kids pointing and laughing, teachers shouting orders, and the three girls now covering their heads and screaming. Dad's voice comes through the speakers, telling everyone to stay calm. I stand there watching it all happen in slow motion.

Stark goes for the lure, making everyone yell again and duck for cover. When Dad picks her up, he allows her the tidbit she earned from the lure. We can never forget that the birds come first. Only when Stark is secured to a block does he dart over to me.

"I don't understand what just happened. Are you okay?" He quickly inspects the bite, but then looks back to the crowd of people still sitting in our ring.

This is very bad. It's the opposite of what we're trying to do with a school group. We want to show them how well mannered and amazing the birds are. I've never been bitten without food involved. It's not something raptors usually do. And now it's happened here, in front of everyone.

"Get into the house, Karma. Go call your mom," Dad orders.

I race to the house and yell for Gavin. He's supposed to be practicing his times tables, but I bet he's reading.

"Get Mom on the phone, Gav!" I shout. "Stark nailed me!"

He bursts out of his room, eyes round, holding a *Spider-Man and the X-Men* comic book.

"What?"

"Mom. Phone. Nailed." I whip off my gauntlet and flex my fingers. How could I have let this happen? Especially after Stark footed me already this month. I still have the marks where she grabbed me with her talons. I knew she might not work as an education bird, but I thought I could fix bad imprinting.

Feeling as if I'm going to be sick, I slump into a chair, rest my head on the kitchen table, and prop my arm carefully across the top.

Gavin hands me the phone. "Let me see. Oh, there's blood!"

I forget sometimes he's only nine. My vision blurs as I try to dial Mom's shop.

"Red Rock Flower Power," a cheerful voice says.

"Debbie? Can you get my mom?" My voice trembles.

Debbie's tone softens. "She's with a customer, sweetheart; hold a sec."

"It's getting on the floor." Gavin points to a drop of bright blood on the cream linoleum.

"Karma?" Mom says. "What's wrong?"

For some reason the sound of her voice causes my throat to close up, and I can't talk. I let out a squeak.

"Mom!" Gavin yells. "Karma's bleeding all over the floor!"

"Where's your father?"

"Out with a class." I'm ashamed of how my voice shakes. "Stark's a good bird. It was my fault."

"It'll take me fifteen minutes to get home. Call Aunt Amy. Lie down. Get Gavin to apply ice. You can . . ."

I don't hear the rest. The phone slips from my fingers, and I slump to the floor.

TWO

In my tree house, I curl up on my red-tailed-hawk bed-spread. At least I think it's supposed to be a redtail, but the colors on the terminal band are all wrong, even for a hawk that's molting. I try not to let the obvious error bother me. Grandma Barritt bought it for me, and she doesn't know much about birds.

Mom, Dad, and Aunt Amy are having a "conference" in the house, which I'm sure has something to do with my doctor visit yesterday. I can practically hear my apprenticeship gasping a dying breath. My only goal in life, besides having a normal sleepover with real friends, has been to get my apprentice license as soon as I turn fourteen. Aunt Amy is a falconer, and I am going to be her apprentice.

Though I'm pretty sure falconers don't get bitten in front of a crowd of people because they weren't paying attention.

A knock on the door. Dad climbs up through the trap-door in my floor. When he stands, he has to stoop under the low ceiling. He sighs, flicks his dark braid off his shoulder, and runs his hand along one of the studs in the wall.

"You're really going to stay out here for a whole year? Montana winters aren't anything to sneeze at."

We built the tree house this summer in the sturdy branches of a cottonwood for one of our Outdoor Classroom homeschooling projects, complete with wiring and heating. After it was finished, I convinced Dad to let me live in the tree house as a social experiment. I promised to write an essay on my findings. But I think we both know the real reason I wanted to live here is so I can sleep in a tree like a wild raptor. I've heard him tell people that I like to understand outdoor things. That I'm better with birds than with people.

I roll over to face him. "I guess I'll find out soon if we did a good enough job insulating," I say, patting the wall beside me.

Dad sits on my cot. "Falconers don't mope."

"I am not! And I'm not a falconer." Yet. Only nine months until I get to begin the apprenticeship.

He smiles but looks away, and something about his uncertain expression makes my chest tighten. "Family meeting in the kitchen," he says.

"That bad?"

"Come on down, hon."

When I go through the kitchen door, Gavin jumps out at me and pokes my bandaged arm. "Does that hurt?"

"Not at all," I say. "Come closer so I can demonstrate how much it doesn't hurt."

Mom is already sitting at the table in her usual spot directly across from the door. She's wearing her purple sweat suit that she tends to put on right after shedding her work clothes. Under the same frizzy auburn hair that I've inherited, her sharp eyes have the focused look of a hawk.

She reaches for me, but I wave her off.

"It's fine," I say, not wanting to draw attention to my wound.

"Doctors sent her home with antibiotics, Kate. Nothing to it," Aunt Amy says.

I throw her a look of thanks, and she winks at me. I might have Mom's hair, but I've got Aunt Amy's dislike of being fussed over.

Dad sits at the end of the table, where he's sat for just about every indoor homeschool lesson he's ever given us. Mom's and his shared look makes me want to run outside again. I don't want to hear that I won't be allowed to help with demos anymore. Won't be allowed to fly Stark anymore.

I slide into my chair and scan the photos covering the fridge. They're mostly of our kid-friendly short-winged birds being held by various customers. I always smile at Tank, Aunt Amy's crazy goshawk. The newest picture is of Aunt Amy's apprentice Bret. He's holding his redtail, Chaos, a week after they trapped her.

And then I find it, my favorite photo: Stark and me after her first successful free flight. She holds her head with the exact same tilt as mine, almost as if we planned our pose.

I found her on the side of a road early this summer and brought her to Aunt Amy, who sometimes rehabilitates

14

injured birds. Stark was so emaciated that I had to feed her every few hours with an eyedropper until she was strong enough to eat on her own. I'd never handled a gyr before. We posted her leg-band information online, but no one came forward to claim their missing falcon.

A screech behind me lets me know that Pickles the owl is in the house again. She's usually the star of the demos, but yesterday I think Stark was. I turn to see her on a perch, shredding a dog toy. Like any other imprinted bird in the world, she craves attention.

"Can you say a word, Pickles?"

"*Hoo. Hoooo. Hoo*," the bird coos.

"That's three, smarty-pants. Where'd you learn to count?" I laugh at her, then spin around again when I hear Dad.

"Well, we have something to discuss."

The smile slips from my face.

"I'm sorry, Karma," Dad says, "but Stark's owner contacted Aunt Amy this afternoon. He saw our posting from months ago and wants her back."

I feel as though I've been footed in the chest. As if a giant golden eagle has stabbed its talons into the center of me. I actually sink back into the chair.

For a few moments the only sound in the room is the hum of the fridge. Then Dad adds gently, "She's from a breeder just across the Canadian border. I've offered to take her back to him."

No, no, no.

"But . . . that's not fair. I saved her life! And how long does it take to notice your bird lost her transmitter? We've had her for months. How could he abandon her like that? And what about how bad this person must be at training falcons? Stark has some . . . issues."

"Clearly," Dad says.

A desperate idea hits me. "What if we bought her? Did you offer to buy—?"

Dad glances at my arm as I wave it around. His look sets a fire in me.

"No!" I cry. "You're letting her go because I got bit? This was my fault, not hers."

"Karma, settle down. That's not the reason." Dad leans back and scratches his beard. "First of all, you know we can't afford to buy a gyr for you. And you know she doesn't like our hot Montana summers. She's built for camouflage in snow. It's better for her to go home."

"You understood this might happen," Aunt Amy reminds me. "I know it seemed she'd make a great demo bird with the lure training. But soon you'll trap your own redtail, and you won't have time for her once you start your apprenticeship."

Sneaky, clever Aunt Amy. The assurance that I'm still allowed to be her apprentice makes me feel slightly better.

"You'll also be starting at an actual school next year," Mom reminds me. "You won't have the same flexibility that you have now, at home."

They all make good points, but they aren't the ones who made a promise.

"I know you want the best for Stark," Dad says, glancing at Mom. "And to see the place where she's from. That's why I thought you'd like to come."

"You want me to go with you when we ditch her?" The walls of the kitchen are closing in around me. "I promised her I'd never leave her. I *promised*." The word catches in my throat. This can't be happening.

"We're all going to go. Well, your mom has to work, and Aunt Amy has to care for the birds. But you, me, and your brother will go. We'll still do our lessons on the road; don't want to miss those." Dad grins sheepishly, his eyes full of conflicting emotions. When he searches my expression, he switches tactics and focuses on my brother instead. "What do you say, Gav? Ready for a road trip?"

"Woo-hoo!" Gavin yells.

Typical.

Pickles screeches, and the sound rips through my head. I want to scream with her. I want to shred something.

"How about you think of this as a little vacation from chores," Mom says. "A fun road trip's got to be better than cleaning the mews."

"That shows how much you know!" I feel like I'm going to explode. "I *like* cleaning the mews!" I scream.

"Karma!" Mom and Dad yell at the same time.

"Fledgling," Aunt Amy says.

The only one quiet in this house now is Pickles. She stares at me, unblinking, as I grab my jacket and flee toward the door.

"You should start packing," Mom calls after me.

"We leave tomorrow," Dad chimes in.

As I head outside, Gavin begins singing "O Canada" at the top of his lungs.

THREE

I hurry out to the mews. It's still late afternoon, plenty of light left. I think we deserve one last flight together.

How could this week have started so well and then gone so wrong? The perfect fall breeze, blue sky, and crisp air from yesterday linger today. But everything has changed.

I'm losing Stark.

Of all the raptors I've known, this one bird has gotten under my skin. Literally—the bandage on my arm is a reminder of how much. I open the door.

The mews is a long building. Plywood divides it into smaller sections, and plastic-coated wire stretches across the top of each enclosure. A corridor runs down the length.

In the first few sections we keep the hawks, then the falcons, and then the eagles. The owls are in a separate mews behind this one. Most of the crew, including Stark, is outside in the weathering yard. It's an enclosed area where the birds can sun themselves on their blocks and perches.

I make my way past the meat freezer, the scale, and the shelves loaded with hoods, creance lines, bells, jesses, and other falconry gear. I already have my satchel over my shoulder, and I stuff a tidbit of meat in it along with my lure, my gauntlet, and telemetry equipment so I can track Stark in the air.

Cheeko's bath pan has a casting in it. The chunky, brown ferruginous hawk glares at me as I change the water. His glare has a calming effect.

"Yeah, I know, you didn't get to show off yesterday," I say apologetically.

At the sound of my voice, Bert spreads his enormous eagle wings and bobs his head with impatience.

"What? Someone else getting more attention than you?" I pet Bert's head as though he's a dog, which he loves. He peers at me from under his heavy brow ridge.

I love being surrounded by these birds. I love the sounds and the smells and watching them rouse their feathers, which makes them look like big puffy balls before they lay their feathers down smooth again. I even love the *air* around them, the feel of it. How this wildness sticks to me. It's soothing and pungent and real, and it helps me think clearly.

But when I go out the back door and my gaze meets Stark's, a fresh twist of pain grips my heart.

Stark bobs her head as I approach, and I pretend the dance she does on her block is because she's happy to see me. Even though she'd be able to pick me out in a roomful of people, Stark is slow to show me affection. Maybe that's why I keep trying so hard with her. I sense she's had a rough life. I want to prove to her that she can trust me. I keep my eyes averted, but I want to stare in awe at her. Once you fly a bird—see it soar free and wild, then come *back*—it's like the bird owns your heart.

In one smooth movement I hold my gloved hand in front of her legs and gather the jesses. She flaps twice as she steps onto my fist and studies me. There is no memory of what happened in her gaze, no remorse or unease. I don't flinch as I bring my cheek next to hers, breathe in her slightly feral scent, and croon to her. I swear she likes this.

She stands bold and proud, and I admire how her mottled white coloring contrasts with the black trim on her tail and primary feathers. Her breast feathers are coarse under my hand as I run my fingers through them.

I counted the days until her molt was over last month. When her new set of feathers grew in, I could start flying her. That's when I could finally tell that she was lure trained. And so smart. It made me seethe to think someone just ditched her. Or didn't care that her transmitter got lost and she couldn't be tracked. She didn't know how to feed herself, or how to get home, or how to live in the wild. She nearly died. How would it feel to be abandoned like that? I wanted her to know someone cared. I told her I'd always be there for her.

"So, I found out where you're from." I can hardly say it out loud. "But don't worry, I'm going to go with you so I can meet this guy and see your mews. If it doesn't seem good enough for you, I'm bringing you right back here, okay?"

Stark studies me and then sneezes, misting me with her bird snot.

"I agree. Let's do one more together." I slip a transmitter over her head and check the signal on the frequency. Her hood goes on next. I cinch the braces with my free hand and teeth. This way, she is calm as I carry her to the back field. Still, nervous energy charges through me.

I cup my hand, making a triangle with the side of my thumb and first knuckle. This is the place a falcon sits, right on your fist. Stark's long talons clench and unclench as she balances on my gauntlet while I walk. I ignore the ache in my arm where she nailed me. My breathing matches her grip. I face into the breeze, and it ruffles through her feathers, making her hop with excitement.

"I know how you feel," I tell her. With a wind like this, she wants to fly so badly, and a part of me does too.

I stop in our usual place. The prairie sage sways in the open field, and my skin tingles with anticipation. I try to ignore that this is our last flight together. A quiver travels up my chest and ends on my lip. *Don't let her see you unsure.* I shake my head and grow a smile.

"Here you go, girl." I pull off her hood, this time fully focused, and watch her take in her surroundings. She looks around, rouses, and poops—shooting a healthy-looking mute straight down. She glances at me briefly before crouching and leaping off my gauntlet.

When she unfolds her wings to their full size, the sun reflects off her white plumage. It makes my throat tight. She is fit for a king. No wonder gyrfalcons were once flown only by royalty.

My next breath hitches as I watch Stark soar. Falconers

aren't supposed to wonder if my bird will come back, but I can't help it after what happened yesterday. The scariest part of falconry is being so attached to an animal that can break your heart in a moment. All she has to do is keep flying and disappear.

She pivots back and hurtles past my head, then rises again to begin climbing like stairs in the sky, spiraling up and up, all around me. I start to breathe again.

I let her ride the thermals. When I fly her like this, it's as if I'm soaring with her. I can almost feel the biting wind in my face. I am free and wild and brave.

Stark swivels her head in my direction. She fixes her steady gaze on me as she soars. I must be patient, but the hope inside me is so big I can hardly stand it. Will she fly higher still, like a falcon is supposed to? Will I be able to swing the lure right, letting her hurtling body get close, but not hitting her with it? There are so many ways to fail, and I want our last flight together to be perfect. I automatically scan the sky above her for eagles. Even more, I don't want this flight to end in disaster. She could be killed in an instant by a passing owl or eagle.

Once she's about two hundred feet above me, I pull out the lure with my right hand and begin to swing it in a large arc beside me. The rest of the string I hold loosely in my left. I let out a whistle I've perfected.

Stark pivots in the air. I watch her fold up and dive. She drops out of the sky, and my heart plummets with her.

I have to time the arc of the lure with her approach, always swinging the lure away from her. When she gets close,

I pull the lure away, slicing the string back with my left hand and swinging in a figure eight. Stark reels up to miss the ground. She rolls and tucks and dives again. I let her get closer, and then I pull the lure around. It's easy to see how smart she is when we play like this. She watches and calculates and swivels her body as she tucks, spirals, and dives.

She is so clever, trying to guess my moves. She flies straight into the sun; I can hardly see her, which I think she does on purpose. Suddenly she summersaults backward and stoops so fast that I gasp at the impact when she smashes into the lure. It's such a savage, primal thing that always brings up my blood.

"Good!" My hands shake as I retrieve the lure from the ground, where she's sitting on it. I'm so proud, though I'm not sure what part I'm proud of. Proud of how pretty she is? Proud that she hit the lure with deadly accuracy? Or that she chooses me over flying free?

When I pluck her from the ground, she's flapping and jazzed. I can feel her mood through the pressure of her grip on my fist. She grabs the lure back with an outstretched talon and holds it with one foot. I let her break into the meat I'm clutching between my fingers. She eats on my fist.

"I'm going to miss you so much." My throat aches a little as I watch her. Her sharp eyes glance dispassionately my way, then go back to her kill.

FOUR

"We'll be gone four days, Gav. You think you'll have enough reading material?" I ask as Gavin lugs another box of comics from his room.

"One-box limit," Dad says.

"But I have to bring issues thirty-seven through forty-nine for traders," Gavin explains. "What if I meet someone who has issue number three, and he wants to trade?"

Gavin is obsessed with his quest for number three. He spends most of his Internet Forty-Five on it. I hardly ever use my daily forty-five minutes of computer time, since it doesn't take me long to check my Facebook page. I have twenty-eight friends. My neighbor Michelle, who goes to a real school, has 781. I have no idea what it would be like to have *that* many friends.

"One box," Dad repeats. "You're just going to have to make a decision. Life is full of tough choices."

Gavin mutters something as he turns to bring his box

back to his room. My bag is only half full since this isn't going to be like a vacation, more like a funeral. I've packed jeans and black T-shirts. Also my hoodie, which is my favorite color—white.

When we load Stark into a tall and narrow wooden box built into the back of our green van, I hope that she will rage. I want her to fight against the hawk box. To flap and squawk and show Dad that she wants to stay here. But she goes in with no problem.

The guilt I feel burns me from the inside out. She doesn't realize we're taking her away. After all my time getting her to trust me, now I'm betraying her. Inside my head, I'm raging for her.

"Text me when you get there," Mom says, handing Dad his phone.

He leans in to kiss her, then she kisses us, and we roll out of our long driveway, under the arch that reads "Beavertree National Forest, Birds of Prey Education Center" in red letters.

"We're already late," Dad says. "I wanted to be on the road before eight. We've got one day to get there and one day to see Stark settled in. Then I thought we'd detour on the way back through Glacier National Park, do some camping. May as well take a few days for Outdoor Classroom, huh?"

"Yeah, Dad. That's great," I say.

"All right! Who's up for 'I spy'?" Dad yells, as if he can change the mood in the car with the force of his voice.

"Me!" Gavin has an insatiable obsession with our family

version of I spy, or wildlife ID. It usually consists of describing species that aren't even found in Montana. But if you can correctly describe color, shape, and distinguishing markings of what you "happened to see," then you get a point.

"Dad, we haven't even reached town yet." I stare out the window from the backseat, the closest I can get to Stark's box.

"Never too early for games, my little wild child," Dad says. "I spy . . ."

I tune them out as I stare at the colorful sedimentary rock and low buttes. The prairie on the left of us, the pine forest on the right.

"Something mottled brown with dark brown tips!" Gavin calls out.

It's going to be a long trip.

I settle further into the seat as I take out my apprentice study guide and look at the photos of bumblefoot infection, but I can't concentrate. Even though Stark is in her crate behind me, I'm the one who feels caged.

— — —

Later I'm woken by the van slowing as Dad pulls into a gas station. I stretch my kinked neck, trying to figure out where we are. The sharp silhouettes of two mountain peaks rise up in the distance. I grab the phone from the console in front of me and text Mom.

Almost at Free Hold. What's world record for longest I-spy game?

A moment later she responds.

Glad you're having fun. Call me when you arrive. Love you.

I stick the phone back in the console, next to Dad.

"Just a quick pit stop," Dad says as he pulls up to a pump. "I know it's past lunchtime, but we'll eat and stretch at Denny's. How does that sound?"

"Shocking, Dad. We only stop there every time we do Outdoor Classroom near Free Hold," I say.

He meets my eyes in the rearview mirror. "What? You saying your old man is predictable?"

I tug on his ponytail and then automatically point to Gavin beside me, indicating he did it.

While Dad fills the van, I notice a teenage boy leaning against the side of the store. He's wearing blue jeans and a dark windbreaker. There's something about the way he stands hunched over that makes me watch him closer. With an exaggerated flourish, he flicks his candy wrapper away, not bothering to walk the few paces to the garbage can.

Dad knocks on the window. "You guys want anything?"

"Doritos!" Gavin yells.

"Water," I say.

When I glance back, the boy is staring at me from under long brown bangs. Our eyes meet, and his gaze is strangely familiar to me, though I've never met him. He reminds me of Stark when she first arrived. Fierce and afraid and desolate. There's a wildness to him that I recognize.

As Dad approaches him, the boy pulls his features into a smile, pushes his hands into his pockets, and stands straighter. He says something that looks like it's meant to be charming. Dad pauses and pulls out his hand. They shake before Dad continues into the store. The boy glares at me, and I look away. A wooden sign on the lawn next to him reads "Home of the Free Because of the Brave."

When I glance back, the boy is gone.

A few minutes later, Dad returns with a bag of snacks. He passes my water to me, hands the bag to Gavin, and buckles in. "Save those for after we eat, Gav."

We pull out onto the highway again, and just as I'm about to ask Dad what the boy said, I see him. He's walking backward along the side of the road, with his thumb sticking out.

"Oh, that kid asked me for a ride back there," Dad says.

"*Stop!*" I scream as we pass the boy.

Dad slams on the brakes, pulling us over to the side. "What? What's wrong?" He whips his head around to look at me.

"I just . . . we have to . . . help him," I stammer. Maybe it's because he's my age. Who knows, we could be at the same school next year. Or maybe it's because he reminds me of a lost falcon. I just can't leave him there.

Dad fixes me with the stink eye, but by then the boy has walked up to our van and is peering in the window. Dad slides the window down, heaving a sigh.

"Hello again. You still need a lift, son?"

"Uh, yeah. Where you heading?" His voice is gravel.

"Just a ways down the highway here, not far." Dad eyes me in the rearview mirror. He is going to kill me later. I can feel his mood like a living thing.

The boy opens the side door as I hastily unbuckle my belt and slide across the seat. For some reason I glance back to make sure Stark's all right. She's perched in the same position as she started in. The boy stares at me from the door.

"Gavin, come up here with me," Dad says.

"Front seat!" Gavin cheers, as he climbs over the console.

The boy breaks his piercing gaze to stare at Dad with an offended expression. He slumps into the seat beside me.

"'Sup," he says.

"'Sup yourself," I say, not exactly sure what that's supposed to mean, but I don't want to sound dumb.

"That's Karma." Dad points to me. Gavin's eyes are round as he takes in everything that's happening.

"I'm Henry, and this is Gavin," Dad says. "What's your name?"

"Cooper."

"As in Cooper's hawk?" I ask. "Very cool short-winged bird—well all birds are cool. But they're cunning predators."

His eyes are hard, and that expression on his face makes me cringe. I've seen it before. It means I talk too much around new people.

"Cunning predators?" the boy asks.

"Good hunters. They fly really well. All accipiters do, they're swift-winged birds. Cooper's hawks are related to sharp-shinned hawks and goshawks; you've heard of those?"

"Cooper, as in my *name* is Cooper," he says, then adds under his breath, "and yours is Crazy."

"Cooper." Dad's voice is tight. "Are you on your way home?"

"No." And the tone of his response slams the door on any further conversation.

As awkwardness descends over us, I shuffle in my seat. I meet Dad's eyes in the rearview mirror and feel a tightness in my belly at his look of discomfort.

"So, do you go to school?" I ask, turning toward the boy.

He stares at me a moment, then lifts one eyebrow.

"'Cause, well, I'm just asking, since we don't. Go to school. Nope. We're homeschooled because we have to be home to run the Birds of Prey Education Center. Ever heard of it?"

He's about to speak when Stark chooses that moment to vocalize.

Kek, kek, kek.

Cooper jumps. "What the what?"

"That's Stark," I say. "She has special genes."

Cooper peers at the box with a confused expression, so I elaborate.

"She's a gyrfalcon, part of the long-winged family. She has a spectacular color morph. . . . I mean, it's special for a gyr to be pure white like that. They can be brown, black, or silver. They're an arctic bird, from Greenland, or Iceland, so they blend in with the snow. And you should see how her color sets off her dark eyes. She's one of the prettiest birds I've ever known. And I've known a lot of them."

"Huh." He's eyeing me closer now. He takes in my frizzed-out hair, my T-shirt that reads "Do Not Make Me Use My Falconer's Voice."

I casually pat my hair to smooth it.

Cooper's gaze finds my book, still open to the bumble-foot infection, and he wipes his hand on his jeans as though the photos were contagious.

"Oh, yeah. Those photos," I say. "Gyrs are more susceptible to diseases and stuff. I had to read up on it after I found Stark."

"Riiight," Cooper says.

"Stark's my bird. Well, she was." Talking about Stark makes my voice shaky. "She was my lure demo bird. Not mine for falconry." As I say this, an unexpected yearning comes to me, and I imagine hunting with Stark. I would have loved the chance to hunt with her.

"I haven't got a bird for falconry yet," I continue. "First I have to write an exam to get my apprentice license. Then I start my apprenticeship with my aunt Amy for two years. We start with trapping a red-tailed hawk. The license allows me to trap and hold one raptor for the purpose of training and hunting. They're easier to handle than long-winged birds, and using a wild-caught for falconry is best. They make great hunting partners."

Cooper remains silent, so I continue. "Once I'm done with my apprenticeship, I'll become a falconer like my aunt. She lives across our road with Uncle Marco, down the longest driveway in the world."

"That's kinda cool," Cooper says.

"I know!" I smile at him, encouraging him to say more. "I've been around birds my whole life."

"So, you ever killed stuff with a bird?"

I glance at Dad again in the rearview mirror. Time to

change the topic. "I'm going to high school next year, in Red Rock. Is that where you go?"

"No."

"Oh. Where do you go?" I ask.

"Are you apprenticing to be a detective too?"

"No, just for falconry."

He smirks, which makes me even more nervous. Behind him, outside the window, something catches my eye. There's just enough time to see a coyote slink into the scrub brush on the side of the highway. But our wildlife I-spy game has been forgotten.

"So, are you on Facebook?" I can't seem to help my mouth from running.

Cooper stares at me as if I've got something hanging out of my nose.

"If you want to know more about falconry," I continue, casually wiping my nose just to be sure, "I can send you some links. What's your last name? We could friend each other."

"Are you for real?" he asks.

"Are we getting closer to where you want to go?" Dad cuts in. "We're, ah . . . turning off soon."

"Actually, *Henry*, I'm going much farther." Cooper leans over the console toward him and points ahead out the window.

"Well, unfortunately, we'll have to drop you off here, since we're turning at the next road ahead." Dad slows the van as he talks, staring into Cooper's eyes through the rearview mirror. "I'm sure you can find another ride."

We stop, and Dad turns around. "It was very nice to meet you, Cooper."

The silence hangs between them for a beat. Cooper stays rigid, as if teetering on the verge of a decision. It makes me tense too. In fact, all four of us sit frozen in place, staring at one another.

Cooper opens the door and leaps out. He heads directly to the back of the van, and I'm wondering if he's looking to come in the back and release Stark or take her box or something. I scramble over the seat to protect her. All I see through the window is the top of Cooper's brown hair blowing in the wind.

Dad unbuckles his seat belt and leans way over Gavin to peer out of the open window. "What are you doing back there, son?"

"I'm not your son!" Cooper straightens and starts marching along the van, passing us and continuing on ahead. Once he's on the highway, he turns, scratching his chin with his middle finger and staring at Dad with a challenge. He sticks his thumb out and begins walking backward down the deserted road.

"Oh, boy," Dad says. He straightens and puts the van in drive.

We pass Cooper as we accelerate. I feel strange, as if he were a wounded bird that needed help, but we set him free too soon.

FIVE

"He was weird," Gavin says.

"He wasn't that weird," I say.

Dad is suspiciously quiet on the subject.

"That road, Dad?" Gavin asks, pointing. "Can we turn there? 'Cause I have to pee."

Dad groans. "Why didn't you go at the gas station?"

"I didn't have to go then, obviously."

"Well"—Dad glances in his side mirror at the figure behind us—"I did tell the boy we were turning here."

He takes the turn, and we head down a bumpy trail that has no right to be called a road. Dad studies the GPS and jabs at its buttons as we bump along. "Looks like this road continues across to hook up with Highway 287. We can stay on it all the way through."

After we've stopped for Gavin, he gets in the backseat with me, and Dad starts up the van again. The road straightens out a bit. I keep expecting Dad to lay into me about making him pick up a hitchhiker. Knowing that the lecture is coming makes the silence worse. Dad must be waiting until we get to Denny's so he can give me his full attention. Wonderful.

"Choose a color," Gavin says, leaning toward me with an origami fortune teller game folded over his two pointer fingers and thumbs. Each of the four flaps has been colored with a different marker.

"Red," I say.

"R-E-D." Gavin counts out the color's letters by pinching and then opening his thumbs and fingers, closing and opening the fortune teller.

"Four," I say, anticipating his next question. "Why do you keep making these?"

"This is my gift," Gavin says. "Predicting the future." He counts out the number with careful concentration and then looks at me again with a wicked grin. "And now, pick another number. Choose your fate wisely."

"Two." I don't know why I play. His fortunes are so crazy.

Gavin unfolds the flap marked with a two and clears his throat. "You will suffer an unfortunate accident involving a turnip truck."

"It does not say that."

"And then you die!" Gavin crows, waving the game in front of me.

I snatch it from him. "Oh, too slow!" I hold him away at arm's length until a hard bump pulls my attention back to the road.

"We still haven't reached 287, Dad?" I ask, stuffing the game in my back pocket. "Think the GPS is wrong?"

"Never," Dad says.

I lean forward and open the console, hoping for a road map.

"Dad, where's the phone?" I look at the floor and under the seats in front of me.

"I don't know. Where did you leave it?"

I think about Cooper leaning over the console. "That boy stole our phone!" I blurt out.

"Are you sure?" Dad turns around and points under Gavin's seat. "Did you check—"

A shocking boom explodes from one of the back wheels. The van lurches to the side, and we fishtail wildly. I grab the door and scream.

"Hang on!" Dad yells.

The front tire sinks into the soft shoulder of the road. In an instant the van plummets, glass smashes, metal shrieks. Gavin's head jerks, and his long blond hair floats as if caught in a slow-motion, underwater scene. It takes just a fraction of a second for this to happen. It takes a moment longer for me to realize that the van has flipped over and we've landed sideways.

The van is still and quiet. Deadly quiet.

"*Dad!*" I scream. "Gavin?"

I blink. Everything is wrong. I try shoving my door open, but it's jammed. The other door is above my head. I reach for Gavin, but my seat belt stops me. I release the button and sag out of the seat.

The van is a horror show, full of broken glass. But the worst part is being sideways. It's so confusing. I can't figure out where everything is. I pull myself up. Glass crunches under me.

"Gavin! Are you okay?" I grab him, and his eyes fly open. He gapes at me but doesn't seem to focus. Then he blinks, looks around, and screws up his face. "Karma! Dad? What—" He starts to cry.

"We were in an accident, Gav. Shush, it's okay. Here." I jab at his seat belt, and he flops into my arms. I'm wild with checking him over, making sure he has all his limbs. My world narrows to only my brother. He's so trusting and wily and fragile, and I hold him and hold him.

Once Gavin has calmed me down, I turn to Dad.

He's too still.

My heart pounds as I grip him. "Dad! Wake up!"

He moans, and slowly his eyes open. The front of the van smashed toward him. His face and neck are bleeding from a bunch of little cuts.

"Dad, the airbag is covering you; I have to get you out."

But it's not the airbag. The whole steering wheel is pinning him to his seat. I don't know what to do. Dad is on the downside of the van, leaning against the door. His window is broken, and there are glass shards all over his chest.

"Dad! Get up!" Gavin starts to cry again.

I raise my chin and hold on to the focus inside me. *Cry later. Things need to get done.*

Dad finally lifts his head and looks up at me. "Karma? Are you okay?"

He's talking. He knows me. "Yeah." My breath comes out like the mew of a kitten. "Let's get out of the van, Dad.

Help me." I pull his arm, and he cries out. I immediately stop. "What?"

Dad pushes against the steering wheel that's bent in toward him. The whole front dashboard is looking like an accordion. "Something's pinning me. My leg."

Dad grabs his leg with both hands and tries to shift it, but it doesn't move. He pushes against the steering wheel. It doesn't budge.

"Karma, you're going to have to call for help. I'm stuck."

My focus is slipping as the adrenaline in my system pumps. I look around the van, confused. Then I think of the phone. It's missing. Then I remember Stark is still in the back. How could I forget Stark?

I lunge to the back of the van, crawling over more broken glass. The fun-house tilt of everything makes me woozy. The seat is angled above me, and I skirt around it to get to Stark's crate. The crate is still bolted to the frame of the van. I peer inside the tiny slatted window, half expecting to see a lifeless form, but there she is, crouched on the side of the crate. She shakes her head. Amazingly, she seems to be uninjured. A few down feathers stick out, making her look disheveled. A primary feather is bent on her tail, but it can be easily fixed with hot water and a crimper. I want to take her out, to check her over thoroughly and reassure her. But if I do, I might never get her back in.

"I'll come get you soon, Stark. You're okay." I leave her safe in her crate and turn to the back doors of the van. I reach for the handle on the lower one and push on the door. It creaks but swings open.

"Karma?" Dad yells.

"Hold on, I'm going out." I need air. I need to think.

We're at the bottom of a sharply steep slope dropping off from the road. I scramble up the slope, which is covered with loose rocks. My arm is suddenly throbbing. I stop to catch my breath and look up at the incline, then back down at the van. Gavin has made his way outside and is watching me.

I pull myself up the embankment. Gravel gets into both my running shoes. The dust coats the back of my throat as I rasp with the effort. Finally I reach the edge and step out onto the road.

Our tires have left grooves alongside the road. With the dirt shoved around and the tire tracks right there for me to see, the violence of what just happened sinks in. My knees tremble, and I drop and slump onto the hot dirt. When I peer down the road in both directions, I see no one. Even so, I scream.

"*Help!*" I cup both hands around my mouth and yell again. "*Help!*"

Only the shriek of a raptor returns my call. I shield my eyes from the sun and look up. It's a Swainson's hawk, wheeling in a circle, hunting.

"You see anyone?" Gavin's little voice calls up.

"No." I push myself back up, lean on my knees for a moment, and then stand tall. From this part of the road, I can't see Gavin or our van down below.

"What do we do, Karma?"

"Ask Dad! I don't know!"

As I gather my thoughts, I wipe my grit-caked hands on my pants and look down at our broken van. It rests at the bottom of a ravine, pinned against the base of a scrubby tree. There's a patch of smaller trees behind it. An idea hits me, and I jump off the road, sliding back down the soft sand toward the van.

"You see anything?" Dad asks.

"Hang on, I'm going to get you out." I head for the shade of the trees, searching for a long branch. Gavin watches. His eyes are big and red, and his face is pale white.

I find a sturdy branch and push one end on the ground, leaning my full weight on it. It bends but doesn't give. Please let this work.

By the time I climb into the van again, maneuvering the long branch through the back doors, I'm soaked in sweat. My eyes burn, but the only thing I care about right now is getting Dad free.

"Try this, Dad. Can you wedge it under the wheel?"

Dad fumbles, and when I see how truly stuck he is, my head pounds. He shoves the branch between his knees, gritting his teeth.

"Good! I'm going to use the console as a pivot point. Remember the fulcrum lesson. . . . Dad? You okay?" I feel like I could protect him with the power of my need. He has to be okay.

"I'm okay," he says.

I don't like the idea of pressing on Dad's leg, but I'm ready to try anything. Gavin and I lean on the branch with our combined weight, but nothing happens. We jump up and down on it, thrashing it this way and that. Still, the steering wheel doesn't budge.

"What are we going to do?" Gavin cries. He slumps to the seat.

That's when I notice Stark's cage door is wide open. I scramble over and peer in. The crate sits empty.

"Where—? What happened to Stark?" I whirl around and look at Gavin.

His gaze casts down at the broken glass at his feet. "She got away," he says.

"What?"

"I was just going to see if she was okay, but when I opened the door, she left."

"*What?* Why did you . . . ? She was totally freaked out." Everything closes in on me now. The accident, the roll down the embankment, metal crunching, broken glass, Dad trapped, deserted road, no phone. And now Stark is gone.

My sobs drown out anything that Dad and Gavin say.

SIX

I sniff and raise my head.

"Karma," Dad says softly.

I crawl over to him and lean on his shoulder. He tries to put an arm around me, but I can see in his expression that it's awkward and painful for him. He gives up and rubs my arm instead. I peer at his face again.

"We need to fix you up," I say.

I scramble for the first-aid kit tucked into the back compartment and take out sterile gauze and antiseptic to clean Dad's cuts. Some have glass stuck in them. I find tweezers in the first-aid kit. They're hard to grip and my fingers shake as I pull the glass out. Gavin has no cuts. The window on his side didn't break.

"I'm sorry," Dad says. "Our tire blew, and I lost control."

"It's okay. Just tell me what to do now."

He's quiet for a long moment. I know what he's thinking, and I don't know if I can do it. I don't know if I can leave him here. But I have to get us help. Am I brave enough to hike out alone? I don't feel that brave.

"I'm going for help," I say.

"I'm going too," Gavin says behind me.

"No," both Dad and I say at once.

"I need help here, little man," Dad says. Then he looks at me. "We've gone over forty miles from the highway, but the GPS showed we were almost to 287. If you keep going on this road, it should only be a few more miles before you get to the highway and find help. I think it's the best way."

My heart thumps at the thought of leaving them. I can't abandon them. But I have to.

I nod. "Yeah, I can do that."

Animated by the fact that we now have a plan, I bustle around the van. Gavin finds a backpack and brushes the glass off it. We sort out what I should bring with me. There are three water bottles in the van from the gas station. I take one and leave the other two for Gavin and Dad.

"Make sure Dad gets enough to drink while I'm gone." I'm all business as I look at him. "I won't be long. But don't drink yours all at once."

"They don't call me a camel for nothing," he says.

"I've never heard anyone call you that."

"It's a figure of speech." His face is tight as he tries to smile. I notice how he holds his head a little higher. He has to watch out for Dad. His brave act makes me want to be braver and stronger too.

I stuff the water bottle in the pack along with a hat, my hoodie, some matches, Dad's wallet, and a small baggie with some leftover gummies. I leave my jacket because it's warm out today and I'll be moving fast.

"Karma," Gavin whispers. "I'm sorry about Stark."

Just hearing her name sends a stab of pain through me, and I almost lose my breath. I feel exposed and raw. Stark is gone.

But Gavin doesn't need to feel worse. "It's okay," I say.

He wants to say something else, so I don't meet his eyes. I feel him wanting more from me, but I'm afraid I'm going to lose my nerve to leave. I wipe my nose and swing the backpack on.

When I crouch to Dad's level, he kisses my forehead and smooths my hair back. "I know you'll do it," he says. "You're so brave. We'll see you back here in no time."

I watch his face as he tries to find a more comfortable position. My insides clench with the need to get him out of here. Abruptly I rise and dash out the door, heading up the scree-covered slope toward the road.

Gavin's voice follows me. "Watch out for snakes!"

That little turd.

Once on the road, I look back in the direction we came from and listen, straining to hear any sound of oncoming traffic. There's nothing out here but us. I look up at the sky, searching for a flash of white.

I'm on my own.

Hitching up my pack, I swallow down the lump in my throat and turn to head down the road, toward the un-known.

SEVEN

Water is an issue. I wish I could take a full drink and slake my thirst, but I only sip from the small water bottle, trying to save the rest. I close the cap tightly and slip it back into my pack. The sun burns down on the land around me. Is it really the end of October?

Brown rolling hills sprawl out in front of me. I can't see past the next hill. A blunt-topped mountain on my right is dotted with patches of pine and Douglas fir trees. Sagebrush hugs the road. And the endless larger peaks in the distance don't seem to be getting any closer. I've been walking for hours on a road with no name and no end.

I take off my hat and fan my face. I wish I weren't wearing black. Then I pull my hat back down again and keep walking. Exactly how far away were we from the highway? The sun has moved across the sky. I didn't think I'd get caught out here in the dark. I can't be gone so long. My feet move faster.

The ticking stopwatch inside my head is counting the minutes that Dad remains trapped in the van, unable to shift or get comfortable. What if his legs are crushed, and he's paralyzed and doesn't even know it? Maybe he does know but didn't tell me. That's why he wasn't screaming in pain. He couldn't feel anything. What if he can never walk again? What if he'll have to live the rest of his life in a wheelchair? We'll have to build a ramp into the house. Will Dad be able to fly birds if he's in a chair? The questions increase all because our stupid tire blew up. How does that happen, anyway?

If we had our phone, maybe I would've found coverage. I wouldn't be walking by myself in the middle of nowhere, trying to get to the highway. If I ever see that thieving Cooper again, I'm going to kill him myself. But I'm the one who made Dad pick him up. The thought makes me ill.

I stop when I hear something. It sounds like something is scuffling behind the red rock ridges along the road. I look behind me. My skin prickles as if I'm being watched. But I don't see anything except empty road. I turn back and walk faster.

Where was I? Oh, yes. Cooper. Maybe I won't kill him. Perhaps I'll just maim him. I wish I had talons—long, sharp talons. I'd rip them up his arm, sink them into his flesh. Leave memories all over. Let him remember that taking things that don't belong to him can put people in danger. I can't believe I felt bad for ditching him.

I keep walking, seething more with every step. Until the road simply ends. It stops at a berm. The pile of dirt is as high as my chest, as if someone forgot to roll it out to form the rest of the road.

I drop my pack and slowly turn in a circle. There are no signs. No highway.

"Bird turds!" I kick savagely at my pack. It feels good, so I keep kicking it, then kick the berm. I scream into the empty space around me.

Why would someone build a road only partway? I raise my gaze straight ahead to the horizon. I can't go back; the van is at least five miles away. And from there it's a two-day walk or more to cover the forty-plus miles past the van to the highway we came from.

The GPS was wrong about this road. But maybe it's right about Highway 287 being close. It has to be right about something as major as a highway. What if the highway is just over the next hill?

But what if it isn't? Should I go back and ask Dad what to do? I stare at the vista ahead of me, debating. Forested ridges of mountain rise to the sky on my right. Flat prairie, sagebrush, and low buttes spread out on my left. Without a road ahead of me, I'll have to cut cross-country to find this highway. On blind faith in a GPS that was already wrong about this road. I almost turn back, but then I stop.

Turning back would be wasted time. And I can't face walking all that way again without anything to show for it. I have to find help. If I go back without it, we'll be right back where we started.

Glancing at the tops of the pines on the mountain, I

search for white dots. Stark's absence is like a wound in my heart. I hope she's okay.

I pick up my pack and scramble over the berm. I head straight through the wilderness, directly toward the red rocks climbing to the setting sun.

EIGHT

My water bottle is half empty.

Half full, that's what I should be thinking. Positive. The bottle is half full. And I'm about to walk onto the highway, and there will be a nice family resting on the side at a picnic stop. They'll hand me an ice-cold Coke and let me borrow their phone to call Mom, and then we'll drive around to our van. Yes, that's what's going to happen as soon as I crest that ridge.

I've been telling myself this ever since I climbed over the berm at the end of the road. The highway has to be there, because I don't have much daylight left. I hold my hand up to the sun, closing one eye to count how many fingers between the sun and the horizon. Three fingers. Dad taught us it's roughly fifteen minutes per finger before sunset, so I know I have less than an hour.

The air has changed around me. The smells of cooling earth are lifting with the approaching dusk. The red color of the rock seems more vivid, less washed by the bright sun. I wish I could get a bird's-eye view of this area. The walking wouldn't be so bad if I knew how much longer I had to go. I glance up at the mountain again. Maybe I should climb it to get a look at where I am? No, it looks impossible to climb, and the last thing I need is another accident.

My tongue is thick in my parched throat. As I think of it, my stomach growls. I shrug off my pack and search for my gummies. I need something to suck on. My hoodie takes up too much room in the pack, so I tie it around my waist.

I throw the pack back on and then climb the rock ridge in front of me, panting with the exertion. Rivulets of sweat run down my temples. My shirt is damp. I finally crest the top and pull off a shoe to empty the rocks. The sun is directly in my eyes, but I shield them and peer down at something in the distance that looks like a dark line. Is that a road or a line of antelope? I wish I could see past the rolling hills.

Just as I'm about to continue down the other side of the rocky ridge, I get that prickly feeling as if I'm being watched again. I spin around. A few ring-necked pheasants flush up and fly toward the forest. I hold my breath, listening. There's nothing unusual out there. Still looking behind me, I take another step. My foot rolls on some rocks and starts a landslide. Spinning around, I try to balance in the debris. The landslide picks up speed. Loose gravel and large rocks skitter down the scree. I gasp as I see an open crevice directly in my path.

Rolling with the loose rocks, I scramble to stop, but I slide right off the edge.

I start to scream. My fall is suddenly cut short. I'm caught in midair when my pack snags on something along the inside of the rock crevice where I've fallen. I'm dangling above a dark hole. The falcon-like part of my brain kicks in. My eyes dart, searching for a solution.

As I swing my arms back, I feel the graze of the hard rock, but there's nothing to grab hold of. My pack begins to rip.

"Don't you dare!"

I try to turn and get my arms out of the straps so I can climb. The crevice rim is just above my head. I slip one arm out but feel myself falling backward. Clawing at the rock, I gain hold of a smooth root. Such a tiny root. When I try to pull myself up, I feel the root tear, and I scramble for a different hold. My fingers slip, peeling off the thin coating of the root.

"No! Come on!"

The root breaks. I plummet into the dark abyss.

Before the landing comes, I have a brief moment to hate myself for failing Dad and Gavin. And then I smash into the ground, all the wind rushing out of my lungs. I lie gasping, trying to find my breath. When I take a painful gulp of air, the sound of it echoes off the walls around me.

I try to sit up, but I'm tangled in something. Whatever has broken my fall creaks and shifts underneath me. I roll and come face-to-face with a gaping jaw.

"Wha—!"

I kick and try to jump back, but something has a grip on my hoodie. I fight it off. The jaw sags toward me. Frantic,

I thrash and punch, trying to hold my breath. I'm in a nightmare.

Finally I break free and roll off, scrambling as far away as I can. My heart skitters in my chest. My limbs shake. I don't want to, but I peek at the thing. I clutch my stomach when I see the rest of the skull, which is attached to a body of long, white bones. Bits of cloth cling to a full skeleton.

After my ten-point freak-out, I get ahold of myself and rise shakily to my feet. I'm in a rock crevice about seven feet wide and as long as my kitchen. I look up at the rim and see that I fell nearly fifteen feet. It's amazing I didn't break a bone. I shoot a glance at the skeleton and choke down a hysterical giggle.

"Keep it together, Karma," I say.

The bottom of the crevice is made up of rock and dirt. Dry as death. Now that my eyes adjust, it's not as dark as I feared.

I have no idea how a skeleton got down here or how long it's been here. Or where I am. Or, most importantly, how I'm going to get out.

"*Help!*" I scream.

I lunge, reach for the light above the crevice, and scream over and over, until I realize that isn't going to help. Focus.

I shake my head and then start a grid-pattern search for fissures to grab in the wall. I feel across every single part of the sheer rock. Not a single spot to grab. I do it again, moving around and around.

My hands are claws, raking across the cold, rough stone. I rake harder, faster. There has to be a way. I jump and scream and claw some more. My knees make a dull thud every time they smash into the solid wall, but I hardly feel it. My breath comes in short, rapid pants. I keep trying to climb until I'm dizzy and exhausted.

When I finally stop, standing with my head down, I notice I've ripped my nails. I hold my hands out, watching the blood mix with the dirt around my nail beds. They throb with each beat of my heart.

My pack still hangs on the broken root. My water. I have no water, or matches, or food. At least I have my hoodie still wrapped around my waist, which is a good thing because it is cold down here. The simple, familiar motion of pulling on my hoodie helps ground me. I take a deep breath and try to think.

How am I going to get out of here? Rope? I need someone on the other end for that. A ladder? Yes, that would do. But I don't have either of those things. A raw and terrible sadness bubbles in my chest. *Deep breath.*

"Think. Think. Think." I knock my forehead with a fist.

The answer to my question is plain. You can't get yourself out of a hole that you can't climb out of. I rub my hands over my jeans and then remember something I have in my back pocket. I pull it out and stare at the folded paper fortune teller. Gavin.

And then you die. My brother's words bounce in my brain.

No, no, not like this. I'd prefer getting hit by the turnip truck to dying in this place all alone.

Keep breathing. If I concentrate on breathing, I won't

have to dwell on what I've done. But I can't escape it. I'm trapped, and Dad and Gavin are sitting in the van, waiting for me.

NINE

As the sun sets, the cold seeps in from the rock. My throat is flayed from calling out for help. No one is coming. The only thing that I'm aware of is Mr. Bones over there, way over in that place that I'm not going near. It's not so awful if I give it a name.

I want to cry. Or laugh hysterically. Or screech like Chaos. I want to curl up and wait for my dad to come. Tears threaten, but I begin to talk to myself. *Don't give in to that. You're not going to get yourself out of this mess if you give up. You are calm, you are not afraid, you are safety.*

There's a pile of rock sitting at one end of the crevice. My landslide brought part of the ridge down here with it. I try piling some of it like a stepladder to reach my pack, but I still can't. Kicking at the dirt of the floor, I wonder if I can dig and follow the fault line to a way out. But once I start to claw at the ground, I realize it's only dirt covering more rock. The entire crevice is a big rock tub. There's no hope of digging anywhere.

The fact that I'm going to die of thirst with my water hanging just over my head would actually be kind of funny if it weren't so deadly serious.

Deadly.

Keep it together, Karma.

My mind has gone numb. I feel a bit off-kilter, as if I'm underwater or watching this happen to someone else.

The sky is deep red now. The setting sun casts loud colors across the rock. It's going to get pitch-dark in here soon, and I'll be alone with crevice ghosts, and I can't bear it. I squeeze my eyes shut, but that doesn't help, because as soon as I do, I see Dad stuck in the van. Waiting. I've never felt so alone and so useless.

"I'm trying!" I scream at the rim above me.

I'm staring up at the disappearing light when I see a shadow fly by. I sit straighter, my breath catching. Please, please, please, let that be what I think it is.

Then I hear a distinct sound I know so well.

Kek, kek, kek.

Adrenaline jolts me upright. I whistle as loudly as I can, and I see a shape fly overhead. A flash of white. A burst of joy almost bowls me over.

"Stark! Down here, Stark." I whistle again. Will she come? I don't even have a lure.

Stark soars lazily above the hole. She's free now. Free to fly anywhere she chooses. Free like the wind. And I'm so far from free that I might as well be wearing jesses connecting me to this crevice. I watch with a tight throat as she pivots and disappears from view. The next moment she's above me again, hovering there. I hold my breath as I watch her fold her wings and drop.

She lands on my outstretched fist.

Her toes clutch carefully on my hand. There's only one layer of cotton between us, so her black talons poke through the hoodie, but they've never felt so good. The feel of them, real and sharp and alive, has a deep effect on me. The tension I've held in has cracked a percussive fault line inside my heart. Tears perch on my lashes. I blink furiously and start to shake.

"You came," I croak.

Everything has slowed to a sharp focus. My blood pumps in my ears. I stare at the commissure at the corner of Stark's mouth, so delicate and perfect. The small notch on the end of her beak, ideal for neck snapping. I smell the dryness of the crevice and feel the ache of my arm.

I can't believe it. Stark found me. She must've followed me on my trek along the road and now has come to my hand. It seems impossible, but yet here she is. It's as if we're both lost out here and cling to each other, desperate for something familiar. She shakes her head and, to my delight, signals she's okay by ruffling her feathers out.

"Your feather is still bent," I say. "But I don't have any water or a crimper to fix it for you."

Stark shuffles, clamping on my arm, and I bite my lip, trying not to jerk. I place her on the rocks. She's come in for the night. Falcons don't fly in the dark. She's going to keep me company down here.

"Thank you," I whisper.

At my voice, she turns her head until she's peering up-side down at me. This signature silly habit always makes me laugh. I almost think she's trying to cheer me up.

"Yes, I noticed Mr. Bones too," I say, tilting my head sideways to look back at her. "But let's not stare at him. I think he's a bit shy."

She straightens and then begins to preen her feathers. The accident didn't permanently damage her, which makes the tangle of emotions inside me loosen. Stark is feeling comfortable enough to preen. I glance up at the hanging pack.

"I sure wish you could bring my pack to me, Stark. Just fly up there and knock it off, will you? That's all it needs, just a tap. Wouldn't that be a cool trick? We need to start training you to do helpful things like that." I talk to her like we'll always be together. Like we're not in the middle of nowhere.

Stark rubs her beak on the rock beside her. A calm set-tles over me as I watch her feak. She's content to clean her beak, and her mood is contagious somehow. I'm stuck in a rock cavern without water or food. I'm injured, and the sun is going down. But Stark is keeping the worst of my fears away.

Her head tucks in under her wing, and I nod. "Good idea."

I reach back and pull my hood on, trying to conserve my heat. As I settle closer to Stark, I pull the strings to tighten my hood. My arm throbs.

It's going to be a long night.

TEN

This hole—this prison—is noisy. It rattles and shakes like bones. The darkness settles over us, and I hear scuttling and scraping, hooting and shrieking. Some insect taps heartily on the rock behind me. The night is not silent.

"Don't worry, Stark. We're okay." I don't know what I'd do if I were down here alone in the thick dark.

Something with many legs scuttles across my bare hand. I muffle a shriek and shake my hand. I slap and scoot and shuffle until I feel I will go insane if I don't stop wondering if there are more things crawling across my body.

The cold twines around me and seeps into my bones. I shiver, curl into a ball, and wrap my arms tighter around myself. There's no way I can sleep, I know. Not while I'm next to a skeleton. There's nothing to do but wait it out. At least I'm sheltered from the winds down here. Morning will come eventually, and the sun will warm up the rock.

Sun. I try to remember what that feels like.

I startle awake with the violence of my shivering. My lips are peeling. My thirst is a gnawing, desperate thing inside me. I remember the survival lessons Dad gave us and how a body can survive for days without food, but not without water. I have three days before my body shuts down. I'll start hallucinating. My brain will drive me mad just before I die. I'm starting to figure out what must've happened to the dead guy a few feet away.

Or girl. I wonder who this was. How did she get here? When? How old was she? Was she an adult, or a kid like me? I don't wonder enough to go inspect how large the bones are. I would do anything to be far, far from here. How could I have been so careless? What's going to happen to me?

I lie curled on my side next to Stark. Soon a dim light creeps along the walls of the crevice. I lift my head and notice I can see my pack again.

"We made it through the night!"

Stark stirs, lifts her head, and ruffles her wings. She rouses, stretches one feathered leg straight out, curls her talons, and extends her wing out on the same side. Her long tail trembles. It's a beautiful, graceful pose. I can't help but admire the strong, pure white feathers of her full wing. She pulls in, bobs once. And without a backward glance at me, she lifts off and soars to freedom.

I jump to my feet. "No! Stark, come back!" I pound the wall until I feel the pain of my arm. Stupid. I am so incredibly stupid.

"Help!" I scream. "I'm down here!"

I slide back down to the dirt and curl up. Not a soul can hear me.

— — —

The morning crawls by. The sun rises along with my raging thirst. My pack looms over me, laughing. That water—just sits there. Even the gummies would work. Something, anything, to stop this horrible thirst. I pick up a rock and hurtle it toward the pack, but it doesn't reach. I try again with a smaller rock. It goes higher, but my aim is off. After a while, I'm too tired to continue.

I crumple in a heap and point at the pack. "Just tip over a little."

I imagine the pack tipping and opening, spilling everything down on top of me. I imagine grabbing my water and pouring it down my throat, collecting all the loose gummies on the ground and popping them into my mouth. But I shake my head and glare up at the pack, which continues to hang perfectly closed.

I'm still staring when I think I see a head appear over the rim. Now I'm imagining people above me.

"Hello?" I croak.

"Hello?" the image responds.

My mind clears instantly.

"Crazy, is that you?" a strangely familiar voice calls down.

"Cooper?" The boy from the road? I'm so confused.

"What are you doing down there?"

"How . . . how are you here? How did you find me?"

"That big white bird of yours is circling above you. I've been searching for you for hours," he says.

Hours? Why has he been searching? How did he know where to search? I have so many questions, but they'll have to wait.

"I can't get out!" I call up to him.

Cooper extends a hand down toward me. I stretch up, but it's too high.

"Can you reach my pack?" I ask. My first reaction is fear that he'll take my pack and leave me here. But I have to try to trust him. "It has my water."

He grabs my pack, rummages through it, and tosses the water to me. I'm careful not to spill in my haste to get the cap off. My fingers feel clumsy and thick. I drain it, feeling the cool liquid coat my swollen tongue. It's like watching the rain sink into parched earth. There isn't enough water in all the world to slake my thirst.

"Now what?" Cooper says.

I shake the bottle's last drops into my open mouth and wipe my lips. "Get me out!"

"Duh. The problem is, how?"

"How about a ladder?"

He looks around, then disappears.

"Cooper?" I call. Then louder. "Cooper!"

My shoulders slump. Where did he go? I strain to listen to what he's doing, but I don't hear a thing. My heart stutters. He's gone. He's taken my pack and left me here. I feel dizzy and put a hand on the wall to brace myself.

For many long minutes I contemplate how anyone could

steal a phone and then steal a pack and leave its owner in the bottom of a hole. What is wrong with this boy? What happened to him to make him run around stealing things? And why was I so concerned about him when I first met him?

Then I hear something approach. It's dragging, scratching, and coming closer. Cooper's flushed face finally appears again. He's dirty and panting.

"Watch out," he says, shoving a broken tree down the hole. It slides to the bottom, neatly wedging itself in the far corner of the crevice. I stare at it in amazement. It's taller than a basketball hoop. How heavy must that be? The tree's branches reach out the top of the crevice.

"Climb up!"

I cram the empty bottle into the waistband of my jeans and then attempt to climb. Because of the bite on my arm, my left hand doesn't grip hard enough. I try grabbing hold with my good hand and shimmying up, but it's too steep a slope. The rough bark rakes across my skin as I slide back down.

"God. You climb like a girl!" Cooper throws his leg over the edge and drops down onto the tree, skidding down the length of it and hopping off beside me. His little smirk of triumph tells me he's pretty pleased with himself.

And that's when I haul back and punch him square in the eye.

ELEVEN

Cooper grabs his face and takes a step back. "Ow?" He glares at me.

"You stole our phone!" I shake my good hand, now throbbing from the punch. "Why would you do that?"

"I don't know." He touches his eye. "You really are crazy. I think that's going to leave a mark."

I don't dwell on the fact that I've just punched a guy who is older and much bigger than I am. I huff at him and look back at the tree.

"Need some help?" Cooper asks with an edge to his voice. "Didn't think too far ahead, did you?"

"Will you please help me get out of here?"

He glances around and then freezes. "Whoa." He walks straight to the skeleton and then kicks it, laughing. "Did you see this?"

"See what?" Does he really think I missed the creepy skeleton lying right next to me?

He bends with his back to me, inspecting it, muttering to himself, poking it.

I scoot farther away. It doesn't feel right to be looking at it, never mind touching it. Maybe the dust of this person's soul is going to float all over me.

"If you're done disturbing a resting place, can we just get out of here?"

"Well, technically, you're the one who disturbed it, right?" Cooper suddenly swings toward me, gesturing for me to start climbing again. "Come on, we have to go. Now. Now. Now." He stuffs something into his jacket and shoves me toward the tree.

I resist. "What? What is it?"

"Later. No time. Come on. Climb!"

I climb onto the narrow trunk, and Cooper hops up behind me. With our combined weight, the trunk lifts off the rim and teeters in the air.

"Whoa," I say.

"Move up—it will balance once your butt gets going." Cooper pushes me from behind.

I manage to grab hold of the trunk with my good hand. We tip forward again, and I clutch at the bark.

"Are we moving today," he asks, "or staying here forever?"

"I just . . . would you . . ."

"Grab it! Now that one. Yes, that's it." Cooper keeps giving me ungentle shoves.

Finally I heave myself past the broken root, and then I'm sprawled out on the rock where the glorious sun beats down on me. I raise my arms up and close my eyes. I didn't think I'd ever see it again. The feel of the sun is wonderful on my skin. Then, thinking of Stark, I open my eyes and scan the sky. I don't see her anywhere.

"Let's go," Cooper says, glancing around us.

I stand. "Give me my phone. I'll call my mom, and we'll be gone in no time."

He rubs the back of his neck. "I tossed it."

"What?" I stare at him, thinking about how hard I'm going to punch him this time. "My family needs it! I have to get help for them."

He shrugs, but I see a speck of guilt flick across his face.

"The battery died. Plus there's sketchy service here. Where's your family, anyway? And the van?"

"We had an accident, and they're still in the van. I'm going to the highway to get help."

The effect this has on Cooper is immediate. The color drains out of his face as he gapes at me. But just as quickly, he ducks his head, shrugs, and looks around, not meeting my eyes. "Why are you going this way? The highway is back there," he says.

"Our GPS showed Highway 287 not far this way." Shading my eyes, I search the distant hills for the road I thought I saw before the crevice grabbed me. I don't see it. But it has to be there.

"Come on," I say. "We've got to get help."

Squinting, Cooper searches the horizon. "Why would I help? You guys ditched me, remember?" He pauses, kicks a rock, and then pats his pocket. "I'm going that way, anyway.

My dirt bike ran out of gas at the berm. You can come if you want. We can split up once we get to the highway."

"What . . . your bike?" This conversation is so confusing. I almost wonder if I'm still in the crevice, hallucinating. "You have a dirt bike?"

"I borrowed it."

"You bor—? You mean you stole it!" At least that explains how he got here so fast. "Why did you steal a dirt bike? Why did you steal our phone?"

He shrugs. "Was going to sell the phone. Had to eat. But it was ancient. Like the very first edition prototype. Why wouldn't you upgrade?"

I have to fight against the frustration surging through me. "Well, an ancient phone would be better than no phone right now, wouldn't you agree?" Why am I still standing in the middle of nowhere, arguing with a stranger when I need to be on that highway.

I turn and skid down the slope, more careful this time. "Anyway, the real question is, why are you here with a dirt bike at all? How did you know I was here?"

Cooper slides past me, taking the lead. "I told you. Your bird showed me where you were."

"But . . ."

"Man, you don't stop talking, do you?" Cooper turns and stares at me with a look of warning. "Listen, kid—"

"Hello, I'm almost fourteen. I'm not a kid."

"Well, I'm fifteen, so I don't need to listen to any lectures from you. You can tag along if you want to. I'm going to the highway."

"You're not that much older." I clench my fists in frustration. Why is he being so difficult? I've never met anyone who made me so mad. He reminds me of Chaos the hawk. You can't push Chaos. She does things on her own time. And to train her to come back to a whistle, we had to first let her fly.

"Okay, I'll tag along," I say, letting Cooper think he has control of the situation.

TWELVE

We slide to the bottom of the slope, but my eyes scan upward, to the sky.

"Give me the laces on your shoes," I say as I shrug off my pack and drop it beside me. To make what I need, I'll have to sacrifice a sock—maybe I can fill it with dirt.

"I'm not giving you my laces. What do you need laces for, anyway?"

"Maybe I can use tape to tie it together," I say, opening my pack. Did I bring tape? I glance at Cooper. "I need to make . . . wait . . . what am I going to use as a tidbit?"

"Make what? What's a tidbit?"

I growl and dig deeper in the pack. "Maybe we can trap a mouse or something." My hand closes around a familiar duck-shaped object. "Ah! My lure!"

I had originally packed it back home with a quail leg in a Ziploc baggie to fly Stark. But that was in my falconry satchel.

"My brother must have put this in my backpack. Thank you, Gavin!"

I tie the tidbit to the lure and then search the sky. "I need to get my bird before I do anything." I whistle and swing the lure as far as I can so Stark can see it. She was with me this morning, and I hope she hasn't given up on me yet.

Suddenly a shadow passes over me. Stark snatches the lure, and I almost cry out in relief. I reach her on the ground and pick her up, along with the bit of meat and bone.

The weight of her hurts my wound, but the fact that she's with me makes me feel lighter. I smile and croon to her, but she'll have none of it. She mantles over her prize, hiding it from me, before choking it down. She hasn't mantled with me since the first weeks. She makes small noises, irritated pips, and then glares at Cooper.

"Whoa," Cooper says.

"She's hungry," I say as we walk. "She's asking, where's the meat?"

Cooper lets out a muffled laugh. "I know how she feels."

After a few minutes of walking, Cooper asks, "Why doesn't she just hunt something?"

"She's an imprinted bird. And she was trained poorly. She's used to people and lures and being fed. When a bird is trained to the lure too much, that's all they want. But some birds are trained to hunt with people. That's called falconry. Right now I help with education demonstrations at our center. But as an apprentice falconer next year, I'll learn the magic of hunting with a wild animal—when the bird accepts you as a partner."

"Well, if she can't hunt, what good is she?"

I recoil. "It's not her fault she can't hunt! Besides, she was doing something important at our center. She was teaching all kinds of people about falcons and making them fall in love with her."

Cooper makes a gagging sound, ending the discussion. We walk in silence.

After a while I realize how thirsty I still am. I lick my lips and look around.

"Why didn't you bring any water?" I ask.

"I wasn't planning on following a bird this far. Or being stuck out here without a bike. How much farther to that highway? We must've walked a mile by now."

I point to the forest at the base of the mountain. "We should head in there."

We're moving west, and the forest runs east-west along the side of the open prairie. We can look for water on our way.

Once we step into the trees, the cooler air is a relief. The smell of it brings me back to early-season hunts with Aunt Amy and Tank. Gavin and I would be dogging—running through the alders to scare out hares for the bird.

I wish we were home. An ache fills me. *I wish we were home.*

Shaking my head, I adjust Stark on my fist. She's getting heavy.

We hike over soft needles and crunchy pinecones. Squirrels chitter at us. We're surrounded by lush pines. Between the mountain, the forest, and the prairie, I think Dad would like to do an Outdoor Classroom lesson in this area.

When I think about Dad, a sickening dread fills me. If I'm thirsty, so are they. Three days. That's as long as anyone can live without water. I left them yesterday, so the clock started then. Gavin would have finished the water they had by now. I need to find that highway. Where is it?

My throat burns. I lick my lips again.

"Where would we find water, you think?" Cooper asks.

"Dig into my pack," I say as I turn my back to him. "I've got some gummies."

I stand still as Cooper rummages through my pack. I'm not sure why it feels so personal with him in my pack while it's on my back. But I didn't want to move Stark from my fist. I'm afraid she'll leave.

Cooper pulls out the Ziploc bag but doesn't give it to me when I hold my hand out for it. He empties it into his own hand. I have time to see there were only five left in the bag before he grabs them and tosses them into his mouth.

I'm just about to kick him in the shin when he hands me the ones he saved. Three gummies tumble into my palm.

"We need a creek or something," Cooper says. I nod.

I suck my gummies slowly as we continue. The sugar rush helps keep my feet moving, but too soon my steps are sluggish. My thirst roars in my head. My empty stomach growls. I feel hollowed out. I'm painfully aware I haven't eaten a real meal since yesterday morning. Was it only yesterday that I was at home eating flax pancakes? It feels like a lifetime ago.

My arm throbs with the effort of carrying Stark. I'm

about to call a break when Cooper slows down and then sits on a log. With relief, I transfer Stark to a stump and swing my arm around. Out of the corner of my eye, I watch Cooper pull out the thing he's been hiding in his jacket.

I sit down beside him, and he immediately moves farther away.

"What is that?" I ask.

He holds something in his hands. As he shuffles, trying to hide whatever it is he's got, loose papers flutter onto the ground between us. Cooper scoops them up, but not before I recognize what it is.

"Where did you get that money?"

Cooper narrows his eyes at me and then shoves the bills into his pocket, tossing a decaying wallet on the ground. "I found it. It's mine."

"You stole it."

Cooper stands. "That pile of bones wasn't using it anymore. Think of it as payment for risking my life for you."

When I study him, he squirms under my gaze.

"What?" The dangerously low way Cooper says this sends a cold prickle across my neck. I wonder how safe I really am with him. Maybe I'd be better off by myself.

"I don't care about your money, all right? I just need to get help for my family. We should keep going."

Cooper gestures for me to lead the way. I take up Stark again, ignoring the pain, and we plod along the edge of the forest without looking at each other. I keep peering ahead uneasily. There's still no sign of a highway or road, or even a trail. We should've been there by now.

As we walk, I can't handle the silence. "How much money is that?" I ask.

"I knew it. Money is all anyone cares about, including you. You're looking for a bribe, aren't you? Fine. How much to keep you quiet about it?"

I keep walking calmly. "I wasn't thinking that at all. Just, I wonder how no one found him. When did he fall into the crevice? Why didn't anyone look for him? It's a mystery, don't you think?"

"What do I care?" Cooper trips on a root while trying to keep pace with me and curses.

"And I wonder why the wallet and money didn't decompose but the body did," I say.

"In open air, the body would only take, like, a year," Cooper says. "But the money was protected in the wallet. It's really not that big a mystery."

With an uneasy feeling, I study him out of the corner of my eye. Why does he know how long a body takes to decompose?

The pines here block out the sun. When we get closer to the edge of the forest I see where the sun is, and it's much lower than I thought. We've been walking ever since Cooper got me out of the crevice.

As we hike, a subtle sound breaks through my thoughts.

"Stop!" I hold out a hand. "Do you hear that?" We look at each other, straining to listen over the wind through the trees.

"Water!" We both turn and race toward the sound. I think it's coming from our right, but Cooper runs to the left. I crash through a large clump of willows. When I emerge on the other side, I'm beside a nearly dried-up stream. The water gurgles over rocks and collects in a little pool.

"Cooper, over here!" I hope Stark will have a bath, but she ignores the water after hopping off my fist.

We both plunge our cupped hands in and pull up handfuls of delicious, cool water. It is sweet and glorious. I'm a sponge, with all my nooks and crannies filling out. If I drink enough, maybe it will fill the emptiness in my belly. But the water only makes me hungrier.

"Doesn't the bird drink?" Cooper asks.

"They get water from meat. But they usually love to bathe if they feel like they're in a safe environment." I sit back and wipe my mouth. Water soaks the top of my hoodie and the bottoms of my sleeves. The filthy bandage on my arm is soaked too and is sticking to my skin, but I'm afraid to mess with it. I don't want to look at it just now. We sit for a moment, absorbing the water. My mouth finally feels normal.

Reaching into my waistband at the small of my back, I pull out the empty water bottle and fill it. "I wish we had another bottle to carry the water in. I don't know when we're going to find more."

Then I remember the Ziploc bag the gummies were in. I pull it out and dip the bag into the water. When I zip it closed, it's like a square water balloon. I carefully hold it up to inspect for any holes. No leaks.

"This will work until we get to—" I'm interrupted by a scream behind me.

I whirl around in time to see Cooper do a little dance.

His knees come up in rapid succession while he looks down in horror.

"What?"

"Snake! Yeah. It's just a snake. Snuck up on me." Cooper sniffs and flicks his hair out of his eyes. Once he has his cool again, he puts on an expression of indifference like a cloak. He picks up a stick and spreads the grasses with it, peering at the snake.

"We can eat that," he says.

"Yikes. Watch it—that's a prairie rattlesnake," I say. "It's late in the season for them to be out."

"So we can't eat it?"

"They're venomous, not poisonous. We can eat it, as long as we don't let it bite us."

Cooper picks up a rock and hurls it at the snake. It coils up, rattles, and slithers into a hole between some rocks. The speed it can move makes me want to lift both feet at the same time. I watch from a distance.

"What's wrong?" Cooper asks. "You afraid of snakes?"

"No, it's not that, it's just . . . well. Yeah, I may be afraid of snakes."

"This sucks," Cooper says, peering into the place the snake disappeared. "Feels like forever since I ate anything."

With the water packed in my bag, I notice how much heavier it is. And how much weaker I feel. We need to find something to eat. But even more than that, we need to find the highway.

THIRTEEN

As we continue through the trees a squirrel scolds us from above.

"Hey. We could eat squirrels," Cooper says, looking up. "You don't have a trap in that pack, do you?"

"We could make a trap with the willows over there," I say. "In Outdoor Classroom we once made willow chairs by weaving the bendy twigs together. I wasn't that impressed with them, but Gavin was so proud of his that he painted his name on it. It's still on our porch." The memory tugs at my heart. I glance at the sky. "Except we don't have time."

Cooper pulls out something that had been clipped along the inside of his front pocket. I hear a *snick* as he uses his thumb to flick out a thick, pointy blade. He slices at the willows and then stops when he catches me staring at him. He grins wickedly and flips the knife in the air, catching it by the black handle.

"What?" he asks innocently.

"What are you doing?" I try not to sound concerned about the fact that he's had a knife on him this whole time.

"I'm making a spear. I'm going to stab us some dinner. Someone has to think around here."

While Cooper sharpens a long willow, I transfer Stark to my shoulder on top of the padding of my pack strap. I can't keep carrying her with my injured arm. I have to improvise. She's not sure what I'm doing at first, but then she shuffles on. I smile at the novelty of having a bird on my shoulder. I feel her grip tighten, but her talons don't poke through. It's way easier to carry her this way. She leans in and plucks at my hair as a bittersweet wave of emotion hits me.

"What a good girl. That's it, Stark. Are you finally telling me you love me too?"

Cooper stalks past us, brandishing his new spear. "You enjoying yourself, Crazy?"

"What?"

He hurtles the spear at the squirrel above us, but it scampers away easily. Cooper screams at it and then stomps his foot. I'm suddenly afraid of his mood swing.

"Freaking idiot! This whole thing is so lame. What do you think—that we're just tiptoeing through the tulips out here? I can't believe I'm out here starving to death . . . with you." Cooper grabs the spear where it fell, and savagely throws it again into the trees. "I never should've followed that stupid bird."

"I'm not an idiot! How could you forget that this is your fault? If you didn't steal our phone—"

"I've finally got enough money for bus fare." Cooper

continues ranting as if he doesn't hear me. "But I'm stuck in the middle of nowhere with some moron who gets us lost and talks to birds!"

His words crash into me and make me face the fear I've been avoiding all day. Did I get us lost?

"You don't have any idea where we are, do you?" Cooper sees my expression and jabs a finger at me. "You think I need you to survive out here?" His chest heaves as if he's been running. I see the tension across his shoulders. The look in his eyes is once again familiar. Like a fearful hawk.

I am calm. I am safety. I keep my voice even. "You can leave and go wherever you want, you know. Anytime." I raise my chin and meet his gaze.

He stares at me for a long moment. "I guess we should stay together for now." He rubs his face. "You say you don't care about the money, but I don't believe you. You want some of it, don't you?"

I'm about to argue when I get a better idea and change tactics. "Okay, you're right. I think I should have half."

Cooper snorts and then studies me. He kneels and dumps the money out of his pockets. He shuffles through it and pulls out a few bills. "I'll give you this if you get me out of here."

We kneel in the pine needles to count the money, but then I notice how dark it's getting. With growing horror, I realize that the sun is setting. We aren't going to find the highway in the dark. I'm going to have to spend another night out here. But this time with Cooper.

I think I prefer the skeleton.

FOURTEEN

Darkness falls quickly in the forest. I can't believe Dad is stuck in the van for another night. When I left I'd never have thought it would take me two days to get help.

We continue west. Cooper trips and crashes into some brush. A string of curses erupts out of him.

"We have to wait until morning," he says. "I can't see a thing."

I glance around at the natural clearing we're in. A thick stand of pines and Douglas firs shelter us from the north wind. "We can camp here."

I place Stark on a flat-topped rock nearly as tall as my shoulders. She rouses and begins to preen. At least she's happy, if hungry.

"I thought birds perch in trees," Cooper says.

"At the center, we use blocks for falcons because their toes need to spread out. Here, though, she's free to go anywhere she wants, so I guess it doesn't matter."

Cooper shrugs.

With the sun down, the cold creeps in. I teach Cooper how to make a fire with the matches I have. He acts as if he's done this before, but I can see from the way he collects green branches that he has no idea.

"You have to find dry, dead wood for the fire. If you pull living branches off the trees, they'll be too wet to burn."

"I know that. These are for making myself a tent. If you think I'm sleeping out in the open with you, you're crazier than I thought."

He's right. We should build a lean-to for shelter. I glance at the dark sky. It's still warmer than normal for this time of year, but weather can change so quickly in Montana. If only I had brought my winter jacket. I keep warm gathering wood for the night, but it's exhausting. I can't imagine trying to make a lean-to. And I can't do it all one-armed.

I slump next to the fire. The flames flick away the shadows around us. The snapping of sparks popping into the air sounds friendly and somehow calms my anger at Cooper.

Longing for something to bring me closer to my family, I pull out the paper from my pocket. When I unfold the whole game, I read Gavin's little fortunes under each number.

You will suffer an unfortunate accident involving a turnip truck. I smile and have to close my eyes against the wave of homesickness. It feels like so long ago when Gavin read this to me. A different me.

You will fall, openmouthed, into a vat of wet scabs. I almost giggle at Gavin's sick sense of humor. Though falling into that crevice yesterday was no joke, and I shudder to remember it. I fold the paper again before slipping it back into my pocket.

Cooper and I both huddle around the flames. They're mesmerizing. People have been staring at fires for as long as they've been hunting with falcons. The fire makes me feel connected to the past and to the wilderness. I glance at Cooper and see he's staring at the flames as if he feels the wilderness too. It seems to soothe him. We sit in silence, studying the colors and shapes as if they could tell us how far we are from the highway or where to find food. It's just as cold as it was last night in Dead Skeleton Crevice. But at least we have fire.

"I wonder what my dad and brother are doing," I say. "I'm hungry. They must be hungry."

"We're all hungry," Cooper says softly.

"Yeah, but I feel like it's making me weak, like it's messing up my brain. I could laugh or cry right now. I can't decide which."

"Whatever you do, don't cry."

I glance at Stark, starving on her rock. "Stark is too light. She'll be too weak to eat, just like when I first got her."

"How much does a bird eat?" Cooper asks.

"She needs a half pound of food a day." I pause. "What am I doing, trying to be a falconer? I can't take care of such a regal bird. I can't even take care of my family."

"You have to take care of yourself first. That's my plan."

Stark shakes her head, and I copy her. We don't want to listen to Cooper's strategy. Tomorrow, I save my family.

"Where were you last night?" I ask.

"A good long way from here." The night has tamed the anger that Cooper flings around. His expression is softer now, as if he's sorry for calling me an idiot. I'm reminded again of Chaos, with her prickly attitude. Aunt Amy's apprentice Bret is still learning how to handle her. But I know how to calm the hawk. You have to let her bate. Let her flap her wings and shriek for a moment, then she'll come around.

"Where is *your* family?" I ask. "Where are you from?"

"Nowhere. I don't live anywhere anymore." Cooper abruptly turns his back to me across the firelight. "Go to sleep."

I nod to myself. The sooner I sleep, the sooner I can be up and out of here. I lie down between Stark and the fire. I inch as close to the fire as I can get without burning my clothes. It isn't just for the warmth. Sleeping out in the open without a sleeping bag to snuggle into, not even a tent, makes me feel so exposed. I wish for the comfort of pulling my soft quilt over me. My ball cap will have to do. I pull it from the pack and then snug it on before drawing my hood up.

The front of my jeans and my neck are warmed when I face the fire, but my back is unprotected. I reach down and pull loose pine branches over me like a blanket. It's impossible to get comfortable on bare ground. I glance at Cooper's form, curled up in his thin windbreaker. He's far from the fire. He shivers and wraps his arms tighter around himself.

"You should come closer to the warmth of the fire." I can't help worrying about him, no matter how awful he is.

He mumbles something but doesn't move. I push myself up to see him better, but my concern for Cooper shifts to myself when I notice the pain in my arm. It throbs with an insistent ache that doesn't feel like normal wound pain.

A falcon's talons and beak carry all sorts of nasty things. What if my arm is becoming infected right now? Punctures need to be kept clean. I think of my antibiotics in the van. I can almost feel the poison running through my bloodstream.

My dreams are full of monsters with bony fingers making my blood black.

FIFTEEN

I wake to birds spread out in the branches of the conifers. The symphony they sing for us almost makes me smile. Then I remember why I'm here, and a fire spreads through my chest.

In the dawning light I glance over at Stark, who is staring at me. When our eyes meet, she pips, and her meaning couldn't be clearer. She needs food. I have no more tidbits hiding in my pack.

Cooper is next to the blackened fire pit. How can he still be sleeping with all this noise?

"Wake up, Cooper, we're going to get to the highway."

"Flog off," he mumbles.

I'm not sure what that means, but I don't think it's nice.

Cooper stretches and sits up. "Man, I'm starving." His shaggy hair is matted to one side of his head. Faint stubble dots his upper lip. He rubs his stomach as if it hurts.

My body feels stiff from sleeping on the ground, and my hoodie is damp. At least there's no frost. I stretch and pull my cap off to run my fingers through my hair. It's a big, frizzy, and tangled mop. As I pull my hat back on, I realize my mouth tastes like something furry crawled in during the night. I wish I could brush my teeth.

I check my bandage. When I try to pull it off, dried blood makes it stick to my skin. I should have taken it off last night at the pool.

"Come on, let's go back to get a drink before we take off," I say.

We aren't far from the stream. When we find it, I bend over and drink my fill first, then let the water run over my arm with the dirty bandage. I grit my teeth at the harsh sting.

Cooper looks over my shoulder just as I pull the bandage off. "Whoa. What did you do? That doesn't look good."

He's right. The skin is swollen and red around the punctures. Some kind of nasty-looking goo is seeping out. My whole arm feels hot. Since I don't have any clean bandages to wrap it in, I just pull my sleeve down over it. "Don't worry about it."

Gathering my pack, I check to make sure the Ziploc bag has kept the water. We head west, toward where the GPS showed the highway. It has to be there.

The sky is a pale pink, growing brighter by the minute. Stark holds her body tense, and her feathers are slicked down hard as she perches on my shoulder. She's light and hungry. I'm full of shame that I have nothing for her. My own belly feels turned in on itself. I've never in my life gone so long without eating. I didn't know it could hurt this much.

As we walk, I try to remember exactly how many days you can live without food. Dad said food wasn't as important as water, but it's starting to feel like it is. My head pounds with each step.

We break out of the pines and walk along the mixed-grass prairie. I spy a cluster of white clover.

"Hey, I think we can eat these."

"How do you know?" Cooper asks.

"My dad taught us. We get lessons on trees and plants and soils. Lessons all about the mountains and the wildlife. There aren't many new clover blossoms at this time of year. Those are actually good; I eat them all the time. I'm pretty sure we can also eat these leaves."

Cooper watches as I kneel beside the patch of three-leaf clover. A few white round blossoms stick out about three inches above the leaves.

"You go first," Cooper says. "If you keel over, then I'll know you flunked that lesson."

I stuff a blossom into my mouth and chew as I pluck some of the leaves off the clover. I touch a leaf to my tongue. It doesn't burn, so I put the whole leaf in my mouth and let it sit for a moment.

Cooper watches my face. "You seem older than thirteen."

"Everyone knows homeschooled kids are more mature," I explain. "Yeah, these are edible." I chew the leaves slowly.

They don't taste as nice as the blossoms; they're kind of woodsy but not too bitter. I hand a blossom to Cooper, along with some leaves.

"I thought you were hungry," I say.

He eyes the clover suspiciously, then shrugs and pops it in his mouth. "Needs ketchup. And a thick, juicy burger."

"Just pretend it's whatever you want. Like, I'm eating yogurt topped with my dad's homemade quinoa granola with sesame seeds."

"You're definitely the craziest girl I've ever met," he says.

"Stop calling me crazy."

"Weirdo."

"I don't want to be a weirdo either. What part of me is weird?" I ask.

Cooper shrugs. "Who cares?"

"I do. I'll be going to high school next year. I have to be normal."

"Um, normal? You say you do bird shows, right?"

I smile. "Yeah, I've been helping Dad teach raptor conservation for years. When a church group came last year, I made and handed out pins of a raptor in flight, shaped like a cross. Pretty clever, huh?"

"Not. Normal."

I sigh. I hate that I care what Cooper thinks. I hate that I even consider him to be friend material at this point. "Well, I can't wait to go to school," I say. "Even though my neighbor Michelle keeps telling me I'm lucky to be skipping the drama of seventh and eighth grade."

"She's right about that." Cooper pops another clover in

his mouth as he continues walking. I follow behind, glad he's not looking at me.

"It's just that I guess I want a lot of friends. I imagine being at school, surrounded by a sea of kids my age. I've been thinking about it so much, it's been like a dream that's far away. But now it's close, and it's scarier than I thought it would be." I've never told anyone how afraid I am to go to school. "I don't want to be the weird girl," I say. "How am I going to make friends if I'm not normal?"

"Try not talking so much, for starters," Cooper suggests. "Then no one will know."

I take his cue. But as we walk, I imagine moving through the halls of my new school next year, with new friends. We'll share funny stories about our families. We'll laugh and joke together, and I'll always have them to sit with. I'll feel like part of a group that understands me.

Maybe one of those friends will turn into a best friend. Maybe she'll like that I blabber a lot. Maybe she's also afraid of not doing things right. Or maybe she's sometimes jealous of her sibling whom everyone seems to instantly love more than her. Perhaps she even worries about sounding dumb in front of people, which only makes her ramble more.

The silence and the thoughts of my imaginary friends stretch on.

"I've always talked too much when we go to home-schooling conferences," I say.

Cooper sighs. "That was about eight seconds of silence, but it was nice while it lasted."

I throw my clover at the back of Cooper's head. "If I'm

so weird, then why do I know more about the outdoors and what plants to eat than you? Seems like important stuff to know."

He waves me away like I'm a fly. We chew on the clover as we keep moving. Swallowing that little bit has me hungrier than before, but I try to feel full.

I focus again on our goal. I was more certain yesterday, but now doubt plagues my mind. I turn it over and over. The highway has to be there, but we've gone so far now— what if there's nothing? I keep hoping that the GPS was just a bit off, and that the highway is only slightly farther than I thought. That we'll see it over the next hill.

I stumble, then struggle to steady myself. If it's beyond the next hill, we need more than clover for the strength to get there.

I'd like to talk to Cooper about where the highway is, but he has already accused me of not knowing where I'm going. If he's right, my family is in big trouble.

SIXTEEN

‒ ‒ ‒

Stark's talons tense on my shoulder, and I snap to focus on my surroundings. Cooper has already seen something and motions for me to get down. He raises a finger to his lips for silence and crouches in the grass.

I scan the direction where he's looking, across the prairie to our left and on to the foothills and buttes beyond that.

Cooper points to something in the grass, and I strain to see. Could it be a game bird? He hefts his stick in the air, taking aim. Does he really think he can spear one? Imagining eating a grouse makes my mouth salivate. I reach for Stark just as Cooper explodes from his crouch. He runs full tilt with his arm cocked back, holding his stick. It sails through the air. Two ring-necked pheasants lift out of the shrubs and squawk as the stick lands harmlessly beside them.

Stark launches herself.

"Ho, ho, ho," I scream, just as Aunt Amy does with Tank. But it's too late. Stark needs time to get height. She circles me, and her head swivels, watching for my lure. I fling my arm toward the pheasants.

Cooper races after them as if he can catch them by hand. They gain elevation.

"No!" He drops to his knees.

As I watch the pheasants take flight, Stark tucks her wings in close to her body and then slices through the air. She misses the first one but crashes into the second with a flurry of feathers. She drops with a few feathers clutched in her talons. The pheasants keep going.

"Stark!" I race toward where I saw her plummet behind a pile of rocks. "Please be okay."

The look on her face is so full of reproach, I almost crack up. She's disgusted with *me*. As if it were my fault they got away.

"Gah!" Cooper screams, dropping his face in his hands. "That was so close!"

"Yeah, but did you see Stark hit it? She's so smart!"

"Smart? She missed!"

"That's how you learn. Let's try that again!"

We set off to look for more birds. With both of us on a mission now, and Stark following in the air, all three of us are on the same team for once.

"Stark has to have a good pitch—she has to be high in the air—before we flush those birds up," I tell him. "Falcons fold their wings and drop out of the sky to catch their meals. Gyrs can also chase down prey, but Stark doesn't have that kind of endurance yet. Falcons like Stark use their feet to swat prey out of the air. I once saw a falcon take the head off a duck in midair."

I teach Cooper to dog for Stark, but he seems to be a natural at stalking. He's quiet and focused. He even saw those pheasants before I did.

So when we both see the grouse hiding in the grass, something ancient shows through our shared look of excitement. There's a reason everyone can see movement out of the corners of their eyes. We're all hunters, after all, born with these instincts. Maybe it takes a desperate need for those instincts to be awakened.

With Stark flying circles above me, and the wide-open prairie all around me, I feel like I can share in her wildness. I'm actually hunting with Stark! The thought brings a smile to my face as I tilt it up to see her progress. I can barely see her now. She's a speck in the sky.

"She's almost a thousand feet high. She's learned so fast. A falcon needs confidence to stoop such a pitch!" I cover my mouth in excitement, then remember what we're doing and peel my gaze off Stark. "Now! Flush the game for her."

Cooper throws his spear toward the grouse in the grass, and they launch noisily into the air. I whistle.

"Ho, ho, ho!" I scream.

Stark tucks and stoops. She becomes a white streaking missile. All I can do is stare and hope. My eyes follow her down, down. She's building speed in her descent, dropping at nearly two hundred miles per hour.

I hold my breath. She smashes into one of the grouse. Feathers explode like a bomb, and both birds plummet to the ground. I race toward them. Cooper whoops with triumph and follows me.

I crest the incline she fell behind and see a fierce new hunter with a hen clutched in her talons. She's panting with a comical expression of shock on her face. It's as if she's saying, "Why is this hen not dead?"

She has the catching and holding instinct, but the killing must be practiced. In the hen's struggle to escape, it whips Stark with flapping wings. The falcon clamps her elegant toes around its head. Cooper moves past me, toward Stark.

"No!" I yell to Cooper. "Let me do it. You need to be careful taking prey from a falcon. There's a technique to it. You have to carefully switch the game for her share. It's called 'making in.'"

I make in like I've seen Aunt Amy do after Tank catches a hare. I approach Stark on the ground. "Good girl. That was good."

My heart pounds; I've never actually done this part before. I have to reach carefully so Stark doesn't feel like I'm stealing from her. Her trust in me would be damaged. As the grouse flaps, I grip its neck in my hands.

"Thank you," I murmur, and I pull the neck apart until it stills. Feeling it with my own hand is even more humbling than when I watch it being done. This part usually makes me sad, but now I understand why we say "Thank you." I understand the respect I'm giving this hen that has given its life for ours.

Stark is busy plucking feathers. Now that the grouse is dead, I help Stark break into the meat by reaching with two fingers and poking them through the thin skin of the sternum. Then I pull my fingers down toward the feet, ripping more skin away and exposing the heart and the soft, squishy, red liver. As Stark digs in, I help pluck her prey's feathers, reinforcing our bond. She will feel like we're sharing the meal this way.

I ready my sleeve around my left hand like a gauntlet and tear off a leg. I hold the foot between my fingers and pick Stark up like we've done at home. Once she's busy tearing at the meaty part of the thigh, I make a trade. In one smooth motion, I slide the grouse out of her sight and, acting casual, stuff it up the back of my shirt. Only then do I breathe. It is done. We've made our first kill together! I may not be old enough to be an apprentice falconer, but I feel like one right now.

I straighten and turn to find Cooper right behind me.

"That was the coolest thing I think I've ever seen!"

Our eyes meet, and I see my own feelings mirrored back at me. We stand there a moment, just grinning at each other.

"You like breast meat?" I ask.

His grin gets wider.

"Here." I hand the grouse to Cooper. "Take the breasts out; Stark will have the rest. We're all going to eat!"

"Um." He continues holding it at arm's length. "How exactly do I do that?"

I roll my eyes. "I'll show you in a second."

I turn back to Stark. "You are a hunter." Her instincts have awakened too. She fixes me with her stare. Her huge dark eyes study me before she bends over the leg again.

"Who'd have thought that bird would be good for

something?" Cooper seems to have recovered enough to be his charming self. "I'll make a fire so we can cook this baby."

When Stark has finished her meal, her crop is full and looks as if she's swallowed a baseball. I press my cheek to hers. "Thank you, Stark," I whisper. The words are not enough for what she has given me. Life. The energy to keep going.

She tilts her head until she's looking at me upside down. I laugh and clean her beak with my thumb and forefinger. She nibbles on my fingers, but I know she won't bite with meaning. She's fed, and it's social time now. I'm happy to watch her feak against my sweatshirt—a sure sign she's content and relaxed.

My arm hurts holding her, so I raise my hand, encouraging her to move. She leaps off and flies over Cooper as he collects firewood from the nearby trees. She lands on the very top of a ponderosa pine, and her weight sags the tip a little. Even though she sits way up there, we are an inseparable team. My heart squeezes as I watch her white silhouette sit proudly against the blue sky.

SEVENTEEN

"It's burning!" Cooper says as he raises the meat back out of the flames. We impaled it on live green sticks that Cooper sharpened to points with his knife. Smoke wafts up, carrying a mouthwatering aroma. I help him rotate the sticks, and we watch the smoke drift along the edges of the trees, staying at shoulder height until it dissipates.

"We're going to attract cougars with this cooking," I say. "Better eat it now."

"What do you mean, cougars?" Cooper glances behind us. "As in the animal?"

I nod as I sink my teeth into a piece of the most delicious grouse that I've ever eaten, even though it's burned on one side and undercooked on the other.

The only sounds are our chewing and our appreciative grunts. It isn't long before we're sucking bones and wiping our mouths. The grouse was just a puny thing, really. The whole bird must've been under two pounds, which is too bad because they can grow bigger than a chicken. Kicking sand on the fire, we prepare to continue our trek. The meat stopped the cramping pain in my stomach, but I'm still hungry. I grab my pack as we start out again.

I look up to see Stark leap off the tree and follow in lazy circles. I smile, a little bewildered. Falcons don't usually follow people the way dogs do. Trained raptors used in falconry learn to hang in the sky to wait on for their human to flush game. But Stark is not trained. Even so, she's clearly following me. My heart is full as I watch her play in the air currents, grab a breeze, ride it downwind, and rise in a thermal. The sky is endless overhead, but she comes back.

"Does it feel like something is watching us?" Cooper asks.

"Yeah." I point. "It's Stark. She's staying with us." I'm prouder than I've ever been in my life.

Cooper glances up before casting his gaze into the trees behind us. "I guess so."

I try not to be annoyed with his lack of admiration. "You think the ghost of that skeleton is coming after you, don't you? It's seeking revenge for your stealing."

Cooper snorts.

"Or maybe you think that someone saw you take the money, and you're afraid they're going to put you in jail." I step over a delicate plant, not wanting to trample it.

Cooper rounds on me so fast, I almost fall.

"What do you know about jail? You think you're so smart. Get over yourself."

He whirls around and stomps away.

I follow slowly behind. My heart hammers, and I try to look calm. I don't know what set him off, but I do know I don't have time for this. My dad and little brother are waiting for me, and they don't have a falcon to hunt for them.

Dad and Gavin would have eaten those snacks from the gas station by now. The three-day clock is still ticking. They must be almost delirious with dehydration. The need to get back to them is a razor cutting deeper with each step.

I pull out Gavin's fortune teller again.

You will survive a cockroach attack, but be horribly maimed for life. A noise escapes me—part sob, part laugh.

You will become a prince's falconer and fly all his hawks for him. If only I could go back in time and choose this fortune. I wonder what would have happened if I had done any one thing differently. Maybe none of this would have happened.

We continue across the prairie in silence until Cooper stops and whirls around again.

"What?" I say.

"I keep thinking I hear something." Cooper stares at the trees across from us. I do the same, searching through the gloom between the trunks.

"Do cougars stalk people?" he asks.

"They can, but they usually hunt at night. They need the element of surprise. I don't see anything." I peer uneasily into the shadows and then scan the prairie around us.

We've come more into the prairie, away from the trees. But a movement catches my eye. A squirrel jumps along a trunk, clinging to the bark. I'm glad we don't have to worry about spearing squirrels anymore.

"Let's just go," Cooper says, with a last look into the trees.

As we head across the open grasslands toward a rocky moraine, the sun beats down on us and I'm glad for my ball cap. Cooper doesn't have one, and his nose and cheeks are turning red. We've had no clouds or threats of weather since we started, but the constant sun can be a hazard too.

I want to ask Cooper about the jail thing. Why he acts normal one minute, then rages the next. Why does he get so angry? Where is he from, and why is that even a secret? He said he doesn't live anywhere, but how can that be? He must have a family. Or maybe he's an orphan. I have so many questions, but I try to be normal, whatever that is, and not ask them.

No matter what his story is, I feel it's very different from my own. I can't imagine not being proud of telling people I live at the Birds of Prey Education Center. At the annual falconers' convention, when the event announcer calls my name through the speakers, he always says where I'm from, and I feel a swell in my heart as I walk out. It's part of me and who I am.

I search for Stark but can't spy her white form in any of the trees or in the sky. I feel a moment of panic that she's decided to leave. I have to trust her.

Cooper jumps sideways, startling me out of my thoughts. I catch a glimpse of a pika disappearing down a hole.

"Watch out for that man-eating rock rabbit, Cooper."

"Whatever." He mumbles a few more things as he walks, his back rigid. Then he turns to me. "Seriously, did the GPS say there was a highway, or are you just playing me?"

"Well, yes, but . . ."

Cooper makes a rude noise. "You want me to think you know what you're doing out here with your clover and your fire and your hunting hawk—"

"She's a falcon—"

"But you don't have a clue where we are, do you? Just admit it."

"Where do you think we should go, then? I saw the GPS before I left. It showed the highway just west of us. Anyway, why do you keep blaming me, *phone stealer?*"

"Enough with the phone, okay?" Cooper raises his hands and clasps them behind his head. He stares at the sky for a long moment with a bleak, lonely expression. He blows out his breath. When his arms fall back to his sides, he seems to deflate.

"Look, I was mad at you guys. I knew you were thinking that I'm just a piece of trash you picked up on the road. You're talking about your perfect family and your perfect life. And then you see me and think, man, we better get the stink of him out of our van."

I feel a small twist in the center of me.

"My life isn't perfect. We were heading to give away Stark. *Stark.* The only bird that would have stuck by and hunted grouse for me when she could be flying away anywhere." My voice wavers, and I stop. "Where's your family, Cooper?"

"My dear old dad couldn't deal with the stink of me either," he says. "He tried giving me away. So how's that for not perfect?"

"Giving you—? To who?" The naked pain on his face makes me want to save him somehow. When he catches my expression, he closes off like a trap.

"You think you can judge me just by looking at me? You don't know me. No one does. My dad doesn't even know me. In the end, it's up to all of us to just take care of ourselves. Remember that, Karma."

"What about your mom? Where is she?"

"Would you shut it for one freaking minute? You never stop. Let's just get out of this place so I don't have to listen to your—" Cooper's eyes bug out. He looks at something behind me. I whirl around in time to see a large brown shape appear from between the trees. My blood turns to ice.

A grizzly bear.

It throws its nose in the air. Even from this distance, I can tell it's sniffing our scent. Then it stares straight at us.

Cooper and I gape at each other.

"Run!" Cooper screams, and takes off down the slope.

"No!" Everyone in Montana knows that the main thing about grizzly attacks is that people run. That will trigger a chase response. Food runs. It's the worst thing that Cooper could do.

"Cooper! Stop!" I stand frozen in place. Then I steal a quick glance behind. Maybe the bear decided to go back into the forest. But no, the bear is moving toward me.

Cooper is getting farther away. Panic clouds my judgment. I don't want to be left alone with a bear. I can't help it; I race after Cooper.

As I run, I imagine the bear is right on my heels. I can

practically feel its breath on the back of my neck. Any minute, I expect sharp claws to rake down my back. Or will it go for my feet? Trip me with a swipe of its paw, then roll me over? It will start at my belly. I'll have to curl into a tight ball. *I will not be gutted like a grouse!*

Or will it go for my throat?

I keep running, pumping my arms to gain speed. My ball cap flies from my head. The pack on my back thumps me with every step. The terrain turns loose and rocky. I try not to slide as I chase after Cooper. He doesn't even look back. I want to kill him.

I glance behind me. The bear is not running, but it's definitely following us. I watch it sniff the air and begin to lumber faster. I swing my head around, desperately searching for some way out of this. *What do I do?*

I can't get eaten by a grizzly. Never during our lessons did I think I'd be facing one in real life. Scanning the sky, I briefly fantasize about Stark attacking the bear for me. Will she even know what's happened to me? Will she fly to my body and sit on my head, waiting for me to feed her? Will she pick the meat off my bones?

I trip on a rock, almost falling. It brings my attention back to the terrain. Cooper has stopped just ahead. He's waving at me to hurry. I glance back again. The bear is barreling across the scree toward me, fully charging on all fours. Its bottom lip hangs down. I can see the hump on its shoulder blades quiver with the motion. Its glossy, frosted fur shines in the sun.

"Here!" Cooper screams, and shoves me.

I plummet over the edge of a drop-off. My arms flail as a scream erupts out of me. All I see is the sheer drop below. The next moment my scream is cut short as I plunge into frigid water. I'm bobbing to the surface of a river, gasping in a wet breath. Where is Cooper? Did he jump too? Did the bear get him?

I see the outline of the bear hanging over the drop-off far away. I realize the river is moving. Fast. I'm being swept downstream in churning water.

EIGHTEEN

Water is everywhere. I can't breathe. Can't see where I am. The shore flies past so quickly, I feel like I'm in a vortex. Every time I try to yell for Cooper, my open mouth fills with water. I choke. Gag. The water closes over my head as I go under, plunging me into that weird world of echoing underwater sounds. When I resurface, all I hear is the roar of the river and my own wet gasps.

I'm carried along until I snag on something, and I grab it instinctively. It's a log jutting out into the water from shore. A slippery log. My fingers are cold as I try to grasp it. I concentrate on digging my fingers into the wood with the kind of strength sheer terror brings. The water shoves me against the branch. I kick my legs, feeling the weight of my clinging jeans. Using the last of my waning energy, I pull myself into a small eddy near the bank. The insistent current subsides. I can feel the bottom with my feet. The water comes up to my chest. I keep going, dragging myself out of the water before flopping onto the bank.

I cough and cough. My lungs are full. Then I throw up—mostly just water but also chunks of something that burns coming up. I lie on my side, retching and trying to suck back air. Finally I lie quiet.

I've never been this exhausted. My limbs hardly feel attached as I stare at the sky and just breathe. I close my eyes. And then begin to shiver. The shivering racks my body and knocks some awareness into me.

This is bad. And where is my pack?

I bolt upright. The waterproof matches were in my pack. Along with my water bottle. But the matches are the most important at the moment. With my wet clothes, I'm going to be too cold to start a fire if I don't find my pack soon.

I climb to my feet and look around, trying to recall every survival lesson we've had. Because I'm going to survive this.

Around me are mixed hardwoods instead of the pines we were walking through earlier. The river roars past, churning sticks and debris along with it. There's nothing downstream to grab hold of. I'm lucky I found this branch.

"Cooper!"

Another shiver racks my body, and I wrap my arms around myself. I head downstream, searching the banks for Cooper. I keep screaming his name until my throat is raw.

Where is he? Did he get swept away? Has he drowned? What if Cooper just kept going and was tossed around in the river and bounced off rocks? The image churns around in my mind once I've let it in.

"Flog off!" I scream to the sky.

As I move along the edge of the water, I see it. My pack!

It's on the opposite shore, snagged on a branch. It bobs in the current. I'm still shivering and so cold my bones hurt, but I need that pack.

No time to think. I wade into the waters again and swim for the opposite shore. Now that I have a goal, the water doesn't seem as chaotic. As long as I keep focused on the pack, I won't think about being in a cold river. In October. In the middle of nowhere.

I let the current do most of the work, sweeping me past the pack and into the far eddy. I'm almost there.

Suddenly it's as if a giant hand yanks me under the current of water pounding over a rock. I claw at the rock. Water is all I see. I can't believe it was only yesterday that I was dying of thirst.

And then the river lets me go. I shoot into the eddy. My knees rasp on the sandy bottom. My arms and legs are shaking with adrenaline. I'm never going swimming again. I want to get as far away from the river as possible. Once I pull myself up, water streams off me, and the wind hits me hard. I have to get dry. Get warm now.

I walk upstream until I reach my pack. After fishing it out of the water, I stagger up the bank. The mud is slippery, and I slide back down the steep slope. But I dig my wet shoes in and climb up again.

"Karma!" I hear his voice. *Cooper*.

After I stumble up the bank, I see him in the water. I drop the pack and cover my mouth. I didn't realize how alone I felt until now. The relief almost drops me, but I raise my head. "I'm coming!"

The river snakes in on itself here. Cooper has wound up in a back eddy away from the current, but the bank there is too steep for him to climb out. As I slide down the embankment on wobbly legs, I see the white falcon in a tree above him. I blink. Stark really is here with him. It's as if she's watching out for him like he's part of our little pack.

"Grab my hand," I yell, lying flat in the mud and reaching. Our hands clasp, and then I'm hauling him out. We both roll in the cold mud, panting hard. My limbs are stiff, and my fingers are starting to curl.

"Are you okay?" He raises his white face to look at me. His lips are blue. Mine probably look the same.

"We need a fire," I say.

We lurch into the trees, and I find a dead standing fir with drooping branches. Cooper struggles to pull out his knife from his soaking-wet jeans. He opens the blade with shaking hands and then hacks at the branches. I peel bark from a log lying on the ground. As soon as we have a small pile ready, we huddle over it. With numbing fingers, I open the Ziploc bag containing the matches.

"Please be dry, please be dry," I whisper. Despite their name, waterproof matches are almost impossible to light when they're wet.

The matches are dry.

Soon the fire is crackling, and we're holding our hands above the flames. My mouth smirks a little at the heat. I made this heat. But my pride is short-lived when I notice my clothes sticking to me. They're sucking away any warmth my body is making. The first thing to do after immersion in water, I know, is to take off your wet clothes. But I have nothing else. The book didn't suggest what to do if you didn't have a nice warm sleeping bag to crawl into.

"The sooner our clothes dry, the better," I say, wringing out the bottom of my hoodie. It hangs down to my thighs. Cooper still has his thin windbreaker double-knotted tightly around his waist. His plain, gray long-sleeved shirt clings to his narrow torso. His hair hangs over his eyes. He stares grimly into the fire, lost in his own thoughts.

I don't know where we are. I've lost all sense of direction. The sun is obscured behind an overcast sky. The tension in my muscles isn't just from being cold.

"Cooper," I say. "We really are lost this time."

NINETEEN

Cooper nods, staring blankly into the flames. "Did you see how fast that bear ran? We could've actually been killed and eaten out here." He seems to have shut down, as if the bear chasing us was the last thing he could handle.

"I've been to wild places before," he continues. "I've seen Yellowstone. Through the car window. But not like . . ." He lifts his head and stares at me. "I thought he was going to get you."

"Yeah, so did I. Thanks for waiting," I say.

"I'll save myself before I save you," he tells me. "Every time."

"But you didn't." As I relive it in my mind, I begin to smile. "You pushed me away from the grizz first. You waited."

Cooper shrugs, then pokes the fire with a stick. He's silent so long, I wonder if he's angry at me again for something. What is he thinking?

Finally he quietly repeats himself. "I thought that bear was going to get you."

I sit beside him, and this time he doesn't move away. He was scared for me but doesn't know how to say it. I can't imagine why he's always afraid to show what he's thinking. Why does he pretend he doesn't care about anything, when he clearly does?

I shiver and lean into the warmth of Cooper, solid and real beside me. He leans in too, and somehow I'm not embarrassed by our closeness. We may not be in the cafeteria at a real school, but I have someone to sit next to. After a while our shared heat slows down my shivering.

I wonder if Mom has called Stark's owner. She must've done that. And then found out we never arrived. She must be flipping out. Maybe she has every police officer out searching for us. But that wasn't even a road we were supposed to be on. They won't search for a van stuck on the side of a dead-end road that we weren't going to take. I'm suddenly on fire with the need to get to them. We don't have time to sit here. I glance around again, looking for the sun—anything to figure out where we are.

"Maybe we should climb to the top here so we can see where we are." I point to the mountain behind us.

We both look up at the climb. There's a path of flatter terrain cut out of the rock by erosion. It's stamped into the mountain in switchbacks. Shrub brush grows along the side of the path for the first part, before it gives way to barren rock.

"We can climb that," I say. "We're lost after that trip

down the river. We'll be able to see the highway from up there."

Cooper scans the mountain, and I watch his face as he studies it. Stark leaps from the branch she's been in, and flaps down to me. She lands on my damp jeans and perches on my knee as if it's the most natural thing in the world. I feel a bit smug and proud that my falcon is sitting on my lap. I glance at Cooper to see what he thinks. He's pulling off his shoes and wringing out his socks.

"Too bad Stark can't tell me what it looks like up there," I say. "I wish I could read her mind. Wandering around down here hasn't worked out for us too well. We need a plan."

"Yeah," Cooper agrees. "A plan for no more bears."

I'm not curling into a ball and hiding from bears. Nothing can keep me from saving my family. I have things to do. *I am not afraid.*

I reach out my hand to stroke Stark, and cry out from the pain. Cooper's head comes up. When I clutch my arm, he peers closer at it.

"Let me see." Gingerly, he takes my hand and pulls up my sleeve. The redness has spread to my wrist in lines that radiate up.

"That's messed up," Cooper says. He carefully turns my arm over to inspect the wound. His touch is as soft as a wing tip. He bends over my arm, studying it, running his fingers over the edges, tentatively wiping away the thin, bloody ooze that seeps from it. Then he suddenly seems aware of how he's holding my hand and drops it abruptly.

"It's infected. You need antibiotics. Your body will try to fight it, and you'll get a fever and get sick within a day. Can you still use your arm?"

I pull my sleeve down, shaking my head. "Not really. It hurts a lot. But I won't need it. Those switchbacks look like a good spot to get up the mountain. Not much slope. We can just walk up. Easy." I force a smile when all I want to do is cry.

"How do you know so much about wounds?" I ask.

"My mom was a doctor."

She was? As in, his mom's dead? Is that why he's so angry? "Oh. I'm . . . I'm sorry."

He looks at me then. "What? No, she's not . . . Just forget about it. That was years ago."

"Cooper, talk to me. Where is your mom? You said your dad didn't want you. Why don't you live with her? Why did you say you don't live anywhere?"

He sighs and runs his fingers through his wet hair. He stirs the fire, and the heat blasts my face. Stark flies back up to her tree.

"Because I left my uncle's place, okay?"

When he doesn't continue, I wait. The silence stretches between us, hangs in the air. Still I wait.

Cooper sighs again. "Last year my dad lost his job and got all stressed out with everything, and we had to move into a crap apartment and we didn't even have enough money for groceries."

He pokes the fire angrily. "Then a buddy of mine told me about a paid job that we could do one night that was guaranteed. But it turned out it wasn't his car we were riding in. I didn't even know that, but the cops didn't care. Suddenly everyone is involved, social workers and everything, all up in our business. That goes on for a while, and I figure that since everyone already thinks I'm a thief, I might as well actually get some money that way."

Cooper slides a glance at me, and I fiddle with my sleeve to make it seem as though I'm not looking at him. Instinctively I know that my gaze could make him feel self-conscious, and I want him to keep talking.

"But I screwed up one too many times. It put Dad over the edge, you know? So he just dumps me off in Red Rock, at his brother's ranch. In the middle of nowhere. It's so small I wouldn't actually call it a town. And he doesn't even live in town but out in the open. You have to drive everywhere because it's so far from anything."

"Hey, I live south of Red Rock! My mom owns the flower shop. It's not so bad living in a small town. Most people are genuinely nice."

"Well, Uncle Mike's already got his own two kids to care about. And he also didn't like it when I borrowed Nicki's jewelry box."

"Um, whose jewelry?"

"I wanted to use my aunt's old jewelry box as a model to make her a new one in woodworking class. We were supposed to think of a project. It was a stupid idea. Since it was a secret, I didn't want to tell her, so I borrowed it. Unc said he believed me, but I could see him watching me after that. He didn't need the hassle of having me there. So I left."

It's the most he's said about himself, and some of the puzzle pieces are falling into place for me. I'm ashamed to tell him that even though I have a supportive family, I moved into a tree house just so I could live like a raptor. Why did I do that? Listening to Cooper makes me realize I took my family for granted. Now all I want is to be with them. If we get home, I'm going back to my old room so I can hear Gavin talking in his sleep through the walls all night. So I know everyone around me is safe.

I keep my eyes on the fire, keep my voice even. "But you're family. He must want you there. Family should be together, even though it's hard sometimes."

Cooper pulls his socks back on. "Yeah. Well, not as hard as finding that lousy highway. Let's get climbing."

I glance at Stark in the trees overhead, remembering that first time she ate from my hand. How her whole body stood erect and proud and wild. She finally trusted me.

I turn back to Cooper, feeling like he might finally be trusting me too. "Okay, you lead this time."

Cooper picks up my pack and throws it on. A small smile tugs at my lips as we put out the fire and make our way through the shrubs. I know that after a bird starts to eat from your hand, then comes the free flying.

TWENTY

We start up the mountain, hiking in single file. The ridges rise in front of us, peppered with scree and scrubby brush. Loose rocks roll from Cooper's kicked feet. I put my head down when I hear them coming so I don't get them in my eyes.

As I clamber after him, my arm throbs with every step. My wound is much worse now that I know it's infected. It's burning me from the inside out. It feels like a living thing under my skin, tearing to break free. I hold my arm close to my body as we climb. I'm thankful Cooper is carrying the pack.

The path I thought I saw from the river turns out to be less of a path and more of a gutter for rainwater, with a row of crevices and shrubs growing out of it. We pick our way along, and pretty soon I notice that I'm not cold anymore in my damp clothes. In fact, the air is definitely warmer.

"I'm starving again," Cooper says. "Feels like years since we ate that grouse."

"Yeah, me too."

"Where is that bird of yours?"

"She's up there." I point above us. "Don't worry, she's okay."

"It's cool she can keep an eye on you from so high up. How does she see things so far away? Like, she was way up in the sky and just hit that grouse dead-on."

"Her sight is ten times better than ours." I'm glad for the distraction to talk about raptors. "She has two ocular sensors instead of just one, like we do. That means she can focus on things far away like a video camera and make it look like it's up close."

"Awesome," Cooper says. "But she's so far from you, why wouldn't she just fly away? It's not like she's on a leash."

"She stays because we're linked. Not with a leash, but we're connected in our minds."

Cooper turns to give me a disbelieving glance. "Right. You're telling me you have a telepathic bird?"

"No, just . . . we're partners. In falconry, you want your raptor to depend on you to flush the game. They know you'll let them chase it and then help them after they catch it. A falconer wants their raptor to trust them and be part of the partnership. It's a sacred thing."

"So can you make her catch something bigger, like an antelope?"

"Well, first of all, she's a falcon, so her specialty is hunting things in the air. Remember? Falcons don't usually hunt rabbits or game on the ground because they use their speed to knock prey out of the sky." I grab at a rock crevice with my good arm and use it to hoist myself to the next ledge. "And I can't make a raptor do anything. Sometimes Aunt Amy and I take her goshawk Tank out, and we spend hours beating bushes, trying to flush a rabbit. When one finally does flush, Tank sometimes just sits in the tree and watches the rabbit run by."

Cooper laughs. I'm shocked to hear that sound come out of him.

"They have their own mind and do what they want to do," he says. "I like it."

"Well, a lot depends on their weight. If they're keen, that means they're at the right weight to want to hunt. And before they hunt again, they need to cast a pellet—that's when they bring up this long wad of undigested feathers and bone. It looks like they're throwing up."

"Nasty!"

"They need to do it before they feel like eating again."

"That was cool to see her eat," he says. "Ripping out the feathers like that."

"In the wild, parents first bring dead prey into the nest. Then they bring prey that's mostly dead, then slightly dead, then pretty much alive. As the chicks grow, they practice handling and killing." I stop talking suddenly. I send a worried glance to Cooper. Am I being weird again? Talking too much? But he's interested.

"Mostly dead dinner?" He chuckles. "How do they kill their food?"

"Falcons kill by fitting their tooth between the neck bones of their prey and pulling on the neck until it breaks."

"Falcons have teeth?"

I laugh. "Um, no. I'm talking about the pointy part of their beak. It's also called the notch. Anyway, an imprint bird like Stark misses all those lessons from its parents."

"I never guessed there was so much to know about birds," Cooper says.

Once we're above the tree line, I glance behind me, anxious to discover how far I can see. The forest stretches out below us, a blanket of autumn reds and yellows. There's only forest and the river. We have to get higher to see past the mountain and out to the other side. But I look back over my shoulder again when I notice the sky.

The cloud cover has closed in and dropped lower since we were at the river. An ominous black band stretches across the distant horizon. That's when I notice just how warm the wind feels now as it blows my hair across my face. Such a drastic change in temperature is never a good thing. I glance at the storm clouds. The wind feels dangerous.

"Maybe we should find some shelter," I say. "You can't trust the weather around here. And I don't like the look of those clouds."

"Come on, not until we crest this ridge." Cooper knows we need to be able to see past the mountain.

We pick up the pace, scrambling up the rock. I brace my good hand against the side of the steep sections. The rock is cold and sharp.

"So, how do people get to hunt with a raptor?"

"Well, first you have to apprentice with a falconer. I guess I'm lucky I happen to have a falconer aunt who lives across the road." I chuckle. "Getting to hunt with a raptor is part of why I want to be an apprentice. But being an apprentice is more than just hunting. It's a huge deal to keep a raptor. They need a lot of things, and you really have to love it. It's kind of like an obsession."

Cooper glances back at me, and I sense he knows what I mean. He felt it when we brought down that grouse.

"It's not hard to love it when you see how good they are," I continue. "And they get so jazzed. Aunt Amy and I get as pumped as Tank when he lets out this excited scream. It feels like it reaches right into your heart and makes it speed up."

Cooper grabs my hand and helps me up a steep section. He peers at the sky. "Does it feel warmer out to you?"

I stop climbing and nod. The black band of darkening clouds has now moved across the sky, as if reaching out toward us. The air feels charged. It has that hushed, expectant feel to it that usually comes before a storm.

A faint rumble of thunder rolls behind us. It goes on and on, grumbling and echoing before it subsides. Cooper stops, and we look at each other.

"Maybe we *should* find some shelter," he says.

But where? We're now in the middle of the mountain slope and completely exposed. As we stand still, thinking, a gust of wind slaps us in the face. We turn back to the rock in unison and start to clamber up the slope again.

My nerves are frayed already with all we've been through. This heavy feeling of urgency hanging in the air screams through my frazzled head. Don't acknowledge the fear. *Focus.* Just keep moving.

I wonder what Stark is thinking above us. She'll sense the storm is coming. Is she worried about me out here? I thought I loved her before the accident, but now I have a whole new appreciation for her.

I just wish she could take me with her to shelter. I wish I could fly off this cliff right now and find somewhere warm and safe and out of this constant danger. All at once, I'm sick to death of the worry and fear. I would give anything to be home on the couch with Gavin, listening to Mom read *Charlie and the Chocolate Factory*, even though I'm way too old for it and Gavin has made her read it a million times. I wouldn't even complain when Mom sings the Oompa-Loompa songs in that embarrassing way.

The wailing wind builds and pounds against me. The loose parts of my hoodie flap against my hand. My hair lashes the side of my neck. The feeling of a speeding train behind me makes my blood rush.

"Climb faster," I say.

Another louder rumble shakes the sky. The wind gusts harder, and I notice then that the temperature has dropped. Neither of us speaks as we concentrate on reaching the summit. I don't want us to say out loud what we're both thinking. This storm is gaining speed and strength too fast.

By the time Cooper and I climb another eighty yards, the cold wind is howling past my ears. I claw at the rock, trying not to get blown back off balance.

We inch farther up. All I see is more rock above us. We've gone too far to go back down. The sky is an alarming color now. A sickly green swirls in the dark clouds. The shade reminds me of a fading bruise. The clouds build and move closer.

A gust of wind grabs Cooper and shakes his jacket. I slit my eyes in the battering wind and bend forward against the force of it.

"Cooper!" I scream. "Do you see anything up there?"

Just as I ask, a thick bolt of lightning rips the sky in half.

"Do you see any shelter up there?" I repeat, but my words are drowned out by the deafening thunder. I can feel the power of it rumbling through my toes.

My insides are jumpy with the need to get to a safe place. We cannot stay in the open with weather like this. I bite my cheek to stop from screaming. I shriek at the sky. After all we've been through, the storm has to change course. It has to.

Then I see the rain.

A solid, dark sheet of it moves across the river. It reaches the forest. The treetops whip around like a field of red and yellow flowers. Stark is probably down there somewhere.

I turn back and practically sprint up the slope in front of me. The rock will be slippery if it's wet. A few drops splat thick and cold on my head. Wind drives the rain like needles into my skin. Winds like these can rip us right off this ledge. Hurl us down the mountain. Our bodies will be broken by the fall into the scree below. I cling to the rock.

"Come on!" Cooper screams above me.

I look up, squinting my eyes against the rain. Water washes down the slope, dripping off the rock and onto my head. My hair is plastered to my skull in moments. Water runs down my face as I try to see above me. There is nothing but rock and more rock. And it has grown darker. We need to find somewhere to go.

Right now. Now. Now.

More lightning from somewhere above illuminates the outline of Cooper. Seconds later, thunder rocks the earth. I can almost taste the current. We're in the middle of it. The storm is not going around us.

With my left arm burning, I only have use of my right to climb. My clothes stick to me. Water squishes between my toes with every step. My fingers are turning stiff again from the cold rain. It cannot get any worse.

And then the rain turns to hail.

TWENTY-ONE

Hard pellets pound the top of my head. They pelt my body as I hunch in on myself. The ice balls appear to be growing larger with every second, making sharp tapping noises above the wind. They bounce off the rock in front of my face.

Tucking my neck in further, I wish again that I had my winter coat. I pull up my hood and cup my ear to shield it from the stinging hail. We're so exposed here. My skin feels raw.

"Up here," Cooper yells.

I scramble ahead to where he crouches against the side of the rock. He's backed into the narrowest part of a V formed by two angles of rock wall coming together. It's a shallow alcove with a low overhang above his head.

"Best we've got," Cooper yells in my ear as I scoot in beside him.

He puts his arms around me when I turn to face the storm. With my back pressed against him, I feel his warmth through my shirt, and the position almost feels natural. I wonder if he can feel my heart pounding.

Cooper has his jacket off and holds it up in front of us, blocking the wind. I grasp the edge of the jacket and stretch it to reach the side of the rock. Cooper pulls it open to press against the other side of the rock, forming a shield against the worst of the hail.

The pellets slam into the backside of the coat with a flurry of noises like popcorn popping. Shrieking wind tries to tear the jacket out of my hand. I stomp on the bottom of the jacket and try to hold it down with my foot. I'm practically in Cooper's lap. The space is narrow and small, but the rocks at our back offer protection. And with the jacket up, we're out of the wind.

We sit together in grim silence, dripping, each holding on to our side of the jacket. I wonder if he's noticing how close we're sitting and that his arms are around me. Water runs off my hair and down my chin. Soon, steam rises up from us as the little space is warmed. The smell of damp bodies hangs in the air.

My hands begin to shake as the adrenaline subsides. I try to imagine we're somewhere else, anywhere but in the middle of a cliff in a storm.

"This is like my room at that apartment with Dad in Salt Lake City," Cooper says. "I had a leak above my bed that would drip on my head every time they took a shower upstairs."

"That sounds about as useful as a chocolate teapot."

I feel Cooper laughing behind me, and it warms me.

"You are so cra—." He pauses. "You're all right, Karma. You're all right."

This acceptance makes me feel as if . . . as if he's really my friend. I resist an urge to lean my head back against his shoulder. I hadn't realized the tension around us until it was gone. It's like we've slumped against each other for support.

"This sucks," Cooper says.

I sigh. "At least Dad and Gavin are in the van," I say. "But Stark is out there in this storm somewhere."

"Man, you're always thinking about her, huh? I knew a girl who was wild about horses, but I've never met anyone as wild about birds as you. You're falcon wild."

I grin at his words. "I can't imagine life without raptors. Besides schoolwork, that's all I do. I'd rather chop off a finger than see any of my birds hurt," I tell him. "One time, when I was seven, Dad found me camped in the mews at Aunt Amy's with Dewdrop. He was a sharp-shinned hawk who'd been hit by a car. I'd snuck out of the house with a flashlight. Dad had noticed me missing before he went to bed, and he said he pretty much knew where to find me."

I pause, remembering. "Aunt Amy says I have a feeling for raptors, like a natural animal sense that can't be taught. I keep the birds calm. Even when I was young, I knew how to calm them, though I didn't realize what I was doing. I think they pick up on our own fears. If you keep yourself thinking happy thoughts, this will soothe them."

"Yeah, you do seem like you're thinking happy thoughts most of the time," Cooper says. "Even stranded out here.

I've never met anyone like you. I can see how you'd be good at it."

I smile a moment in shocked silence. He quickly adds, "It was cool to see you call that bird down with the thing you swung in the air."

"I've always been pretty good with the lure. Lure training is like a dance with the bird. You let them get just close enough, they pivot and twist and dive, and then you pivot the lure with them. It's important to get the timing right so you don't accidentally hit them. You have to feel them moving. The birds love it. You can see it in their expressions. It's good exercise, and Dad has let me do it for the demos since I got better than him. But once I'm an apprentice, I'll only use a lure to call a bird down or away from danger. We train our raptors through hunting. I'm hoping to be a good falconer. It's in my blood."

"Well, I wouldn't worry about Stark being out there," he says. "She's a bird. Don't birds hide from storms all the time?"

"I'm more worried about my dad and brother," I admit.

Cooper sniffs and rubs his nose on my shoulder, since his hand is busy holding up the jacket.

"Hey! Keep your snot to yourself." I turn and grin at him, and he grins back.

"Your family's safe in the van," he says. "They've got more protection than we do."

I listen to the hail. Hope shoots through me, something I haven't felt for days. "At least they can melt this hail, and then they'll have something to drink," I say.

Three days. They have three days to live without water.

But this thought leads me to notice the shadows in our little fort. They're growing, and it's not just because the storm has made everything darker. Nighttime is approaching. How have we spent another whole day out here?

"Cooper! It's late." We're going to have to spend the night. Suddenly my breath is squeezed from me as if something heavy landed on my chest. "That makes three nights. I've been gone for *three nights*, Cooper! I told Dad I'd get help!" I feel flayed to the bone.

Cooper collects me in a stronger grip around my shoulders. I push at him, but he holds on. "*Shhh*," he says in my ear. "You can't go anywhere right now."

"And . . . oh, no!" I squirm, fumble behind me, and reach into my back pocket. The fortune teller is a sopping gob of paper, thanks to my journey down the river. "It's ruined! Gavin made this!" I feel myself starting to flap around like a bating hawk. My vision narrows and focuses on the space between the rock and Cooper's jacket. Sheets of hail rush into our cave and fling sideways like my thoughts.

"I abandoned them!" I scream, struggling to get up.

"No, you didn't, Karma. You went for help. We're going to get help."

But I hardly hear him. I lash out, kicking and flailing, needing to get up, to do *something*. My injured arm connects with Cooper's jaw, and the instant pain is like a white bolt of lightning shooting through the center of me. It knocks me back, breathless.

Cooper holds me while our dimming rock cave spins

around my head. The pain engulfs me. I welcome it. I'm wrapped up as it pushes out every other thought in my head. Finally it subsides to a pounding pulse reaching to my elbow. By the time I can sit up, I feel more like myself and look around the tiny space we're in.

"*Shhh*, be calm. Be calm." Cooper's words register deep inside me. I wipe my face, shaky and ashamed.

Cooper loosens his grip. "You good?"

"No," I whisper.

"Can you move off my foot a little? It's asleep."

"Oh." I shift and we find our spots, with me leaning my back into him. We brace the jacket again. My heart still pounds from my panic. I swallow and close my eyes. I need to think about something else.

"If my friends could see me now." Cooper snorts. "I'm a long way from Salt Lake City," he says, as if he knows I need a distraction. "I miss the city. My dad still lives there."

Another fury of hail gusts against the jacket, and Cooper braces again.

"And my mom, well, she's in jail," he barely whispers.

"Why is your mom . . . ?" It's beyond my comprehension that his mom would be in jail. "What did she do? I thought you said she was a doctor."

"Yup, 'til she hit someone while driving when she was wasted. Or was she stoned? Stoned and wasted? The details are murky."

I turn my head toward Cooper. I can see him in the dim light as he stares ahead. His bottom lip quivers, but his expression is hard.

"Cooper." It's all I can manage to say.

Cooper makes an impatient gesture with his hand. The jacket flicks up at the motion. "The stupid thing was, she's not in for the accident, but for stealing stuff."

"You mean, like stealing phones and dirt bikes? That sort of thing?"

Cooper goes very still. The silence stretches for a long time, but I don't give in to fill it.

Finally he says, so softly I can barely hear, "Yeah."

The storm continues to rage outside our little crevice. Cooper and I take turns holding up the jacket against the wind. We huddle together on the cold rock and count the minutes until it ends.

There are many minutes in a hailstorm.

TWENTY-TWO

The summit is just ahead. We've been climbing this ice-covered rock since it was light enough to see, and we're almost there. Puffs of vapor hang in front of my face each time I breathe. The temperature has plummeted since the storm blew through. I'm glad for the exercise of the climb to keep me warm, but my fingers are freezing. My stomach pinches, and I glance at Cooper. He seems even worse off than me.

We drank the water that was left in the bottle, then poured the water from the Ziploc bag to refill it. Now we've almost finished that too. Collecting the hail hadn't given us nearly as much water as I'd thought.

The rim is just a few more steps away. Then we'll be able to see over this mountain. We'll be able to see for miles in every direction. Surely we'll see the highway from here. I keep thinking back to the GPS when Dad showed me the map. I glanced at it quickly. I trusted him when he said the highway was not far, and I've been stubbornly fixated on it ever since.

Gavin must've been terrified during the storm. I know he hates thunder, though lately he hasn't wanted to admit it. At home, Mom takes out her fiddle during storms, and we clap and stomp around the house, trying to make more noise than the thunder. But Mom wasn't there with her fiddle, so I don't think much would've distracted Gavin.

I slip off a rock. The abrupt movement sears down my arm. I suck in a breath and focus back to where we are. Almost there.

Cooper scrambles up before me and stops suddenly. His shoulders sag, and my heart sinks to my toes.

"What? What do you see? Is it the highway?"

I climb up beside him, and then I'm staring across a flat, open field. I suck in a breath. We still can't see the other side. We have to get across the mountaintop first. I try to choke down the bitter frustration.

"Come *on*!" Cooper kicks a rock back down the slope we've just climbed up. "Will this never end? I'm so hungry! My stomach feels like it's being twisted in a vise. I'd give anything for some fries right now."

A familiar feeling of being watched goes through me, and I look up. Stark flies overhead, circling and soaring effortlessly. I pull out the lure and swing it high. Even though it only has the leftover foot from the grouse tied to it, she goes for it immediately.

"You missed the party," I tell her as she lands. "There was music and dancing and quail; you would have loved it."

The pinch from her talons as I get her to step onto my sleeve-covered fist makes me sigh with relief. Of course she found me.

"Yeah, and we had fries and bacon cheeseburgers," Cooper tells Stark.

Stark rouses as if to say we're both nuts. "I wish you could tell me how far we are from the highway," I say.

Cooper watches her with interest. "You think she wants to hunt again?"

"Yes, of course. See how tense she is, and her expression? She's all business. She wants to fly."

"How can you even tell? She always has the same expression. She's got that mad face like she's always glaring at me," Cooper says.

I study Stark and notice how her mouth at the corner is set slightly downward, as if she's frowning. Her dark eyes, under heavy brows, are deep in thought. She shoots out a mute, and suddenly I'm wearing the same worried frown as her.

"Let's try to flush something out as we cross the mountaintop," I say. "Her mute—I mean, her poop—is dark green. She needs to eat."

"*She* needs to?"

"Stay on my right as we look for a slip for her," I say, hoping for this hunting opportunity.

We head across, eyes down, focused on finding grouse, pheasants, or other game birds—anything that we can eat. I don't see anything but golden grasses, lichen, some erratic boulders strewn here and there, and a ridge on the right with red sediments layered in the rock.

We wander in slightly different directions through the grass. Every fiber in my body is screaming to hurry up and find the highway, but I also realize we need to eat. From the corner of my eye, I see Cooper suddenly freeze. He thrusts his fist in the air. Even though I don't see what he sees, I notice Stark tense as well. She leaps off my fist and begins to pump her wings.

"Wait for her to get higher," I call to Cooper.

I glance at Stark circling above, watching my every move, and I let myself forget about all the bad things that have happened until now. She came to me again, and she's going to help us eat, if we can find her some prey.

I feel so much emotion. Out here, everything feels like *more*.

When she's near a thousand feet, I nod at Cooper. He lunges toward a thicket and disappears. I hear splashes and cursing. He's found a pond.

I race toward him to see him flapping at two stubborn pintails refusing to lift. They glance nervously at the sky. At the predator above that is more dangerous than the two of us. We whoop at them, but it takes Cooper charging into the icy water before they flush.

"Ho, ho, ho!" I yell, my eyes to the sky.

My stomach is in knots as I imagine Stark chasing these ducks for a long way off. This is why falconers use telemetry to track gyrfalcons. They usually chase prey for miles. This was a bad idea. What am I even doing, pretending to know how to hunt with such an intelligent raptor as a gyr when I don't even have my own redtail yet? Red-tailed hawks are much easier to train and less complicated for a beginner like me.

Stark turns and plunges into a magnificent stoop. There's no way she's going to catch a pintail on her first try. She misses, wheels with incredible speed, and gets above the pintails again. She dives diagonally, directly at the drake—the larger pintail. Cooper gasps when we hear the whack of impact.

The drake tumbles.

Cooper cheers.

I pump my fist in the air in answer, and we grin at each other across the shrubs. It's even more thrilling sharing this with Cooper. To see him so excited by the hunt.

I race to where Stark is rolling on the ground, panting, battling the drake. Dread fills me. This is where falcons get damaged. But Stark remembers what I did last time and is waiting for me to fix it again.

I reach in like I've watched Aunt Amy do so many times and grasp the beautiful, slender, long neck of the pintail. "Thank you," I say, giving the neck a quick jerk. The drake stops struggling.

I'm tense as I make the trade, offering Stark a leg as I smoothly move the duck away from her view. Only then can I relax and think about what we've just accomplished.

When I've flown birds at home, it was always for them. It was exercise and for conditioning and training. Even out dogging with Aunt Amy and Tank, it was to watch the bird hunt. This is entirely different. Hunting with Stark—and how much hinges on her success—brings the whole thing into a different focus for me. It's so primal. I have a fierce and completely free hunter perched on my fist, and it makes me feel savage with pride.

Cooper approaches, and we both watch Stark pluck and eat the piece I hold between my fingers. Once she's finished, I wait for her rouse, and then I tilt my head at Cooper. "Do you want to hold her?"

With a dead-serious expression on his face, Cooper takes in a quick breath and nods.

"Take off your jacket and wrap it around your left hand. It's my turn to make a fire. Don't be afraid. You are safety."

Cooper's eyes widen as Stark hops onto his outstretched fist.

"And don't stare directly at her. She's a predator and prefers to do the looking."

I'm more nervous than I let on, but I don't want to freak him out by telling him to relax. I'm not sure why I try it, but the look on Cooper's face makes me glad I did. Someone who is basically my own age understands this passion. It makes me feel less weird.

Despite my advice, boy and falcon stare at each other. It's such an intense moment; I hold my breath so as not to disturb it. Maybe Stark senses Cooper was lost like she was. Either way, there is a kinship between them.

Then I notice Cooper nervously twitching. He's not always the confident and bossy kid he tries to be. He moves to pet her but then hesitates, which is possibly the worst thing he could do.

"Cooper, don't—"

Stark steps off the jacket and clutches his bare wrist with her talon.

"Don't move!" I say.

And he doesn't. Surprisingly, he doesn't flinch or yell. He winces, and then a goofy smile breaks out on his face.

Stark releases her clasp, bobs her head, and flies off.

"Ow," Cooper says. He looks at his wrist, still grinning like a madman. "That was sort of awesome."

"Sorry, I forgot to mention she's footed me a couple times. That's from poor training. She still hasn't kicked some bad manners. Raptors don't like hesitation or sudden movements. If you're going to do something, just do it," I explain.

"Awe. Some."

"I think you're swelling, actually. Did she break skin?"

"Did you see that?" he continues. "I think she likes me."

"Um, yeah. That's definitely going to bruise," I say.

"That's what I call a *grip*. I have to try that again."

"And you call *me* weird!" I give Cooper a look but then grin with him. "It's pretty awesome, isn't it?"

We stand, beaming at each other like Stark-loving lunatics.

TWENTY-THREE

"So you've been gripped with her claws before?" Cooper asks as we lick our fingers.

"All of us have at some point," I admit. "Not with claws, though. Talons."

The meat burns our fingers as we scarf it down, and the juice runs down our chins.

"It's not fun getting footed," I continue. "And it's worse getting footed by a hawk. They have an even stronger grip that crushes and bruises for, like, a week. The key is to not react. You were perfect."

Cooper's eyes shine. "I feel sort of . . . I don't know. Like she sees me. Like I'm worthy enough to be seen." He shakes his head. "Ah, that sounds dumb. I can't explain it."

I watch him, feeling a little smug at the enlightened expression on his face. "I do know, Cooper. I've been around raptors all my life, and I've seen other people get introduced to birds of prey. For some, it's just a cool thing to see a raptor so close, but for others, it changes them."

We both glance at Stark, sitting on a log next to my pack, making contented little *chip, chip, chip* noises. She picks her toes clean, telling me how she feels about being here. As long as we keep hunting and she gets to eat, I bet she'd prefer to stay out here, roaming the mountains.

"Last time we did this, it attracted something I don't want to see again," Cooper says, looking around. "We should go before . . . you know, bears."

Standing, I wipe my good hand on my pants. I've been cradling my left most of the day, and it pulses with my heartbeat. The skin is tight and hot.

"Yeah. Let's get across so we can finally find where that highway is. We have to see something."

As we stand, a cold wind blows over the mountain. Up here, the air feels heavy with something. I can smell it: snow.

We hurry over the rocky terrain. The impending winter weather nips at our heels. I burrow into my hoodie. We could not have lasted this long if it had snowed before. So much for the warm spell.

We have no shelter, and no warm clothes. We're completely unprepared for cold weather. Fall and winter storms in Montana are serious, especially out here in the mountains. If we're still up here when it snows, we're as good as dead. I try to turn my mind to something positive. I'm so tired of everything that I've carried with me for days.

"You have a great eye for hunting," I tell Cooper. "You saw the grouse and the ducks and flushed them both. I didn't even see them 'til you made them move."

Cooper flushes crimson and looks down. He shrugs but remains silent.

"How did you see them?" I ask. "Have you hunted before?"

"No." Cooper seems to be trying to look disinterested, but this time he's failing. It's the first time I've seen him walk with such smooth grace. His hair blows in the breeze over his collar. His little secret smile isn't fooling anyone here. He's pleased with the compliment.

"I'd never gone hunting before all this," he continues, "but I think I could like it."

As we make our way across the flat mountaintop, Stark perches on the shoulder pad of my backpack and pulls at my hair.

The closer we get to the rim, the more anxious I feel. Will we finally be able to see where we are, or will there be something else to block our view? Endless rock? Or maybe we'll reach the ledge, look down, and see the highway just below, cars speeding along, people everywhere. Maybe there's a store right beside the highway. We can make a phone call, buy food, buy all the water we want. I still have Dad's wallet in the bottom of the pack.

Thoughts of Dad and Gavin overwhelm me. What has become of them while I've been out here? What is Gavin doing right now? When I think of calling Mom, the thought of hearing her voice and telling her I'm safe makes me dizzy.

In fact, as we speed up toward the rim, I notice it's more than my thoughts that are swirling around. The ground seems to sway a little too. A swell of nausea rises in me.

Feeling hot, I put a hand over my mouth. My steps are becoming uneven. My hair sticks to my head in damp strings. Cooper mentioned there could be a fever from my infection, and I think it's creeping up on me. My whole head feels like it's on fire.

I have to keep going. I stand straighter and walk with new purpose.

Stark leaps off my shoulder and soars ahead. I think of the reason we took this trip. We're taking Stark to her breeder. As hard as it was to imagine losing her before our trip, it now feels like a part of me will die inside. After all we've been through together, I can't give her up. She saved my life. We have a bond that I didn't fully recognize before. How am I going to leave her there and walk away from her? When I look for her again, Stark disappears over the ridge.

It's just ahead now. I can see it drop off past that last rock as I break into a run. My arm is in agony. A fiery pain slices my skin with each movement.

But it doesn't matter now. Finally, finally, we're going to see where we are.

I crest the ridge a step before Cooper. I look down.

"There's a road!" I yell, hopping up and down. I see Cooper's eyes narrow, and I look more closely.

Studying the lay of the land, the road is somehow familiar. My gaze follows it until I see something glinting in the sun. When I realize what it is, my whole body deflates like I've been stuck with a knife.

"It's your van," Cooper says. "We've been walking in a circle."

TWENTY-FOUR

"What?" My mouth falls open as I stare at the road that I started on. "How did this happen? This is impossible."

I've heard that people who are lost end up walking in circles, but I've never understood how someone does that. Can't they see the sun? We've been walking west this whole time. And the mountain stayed at our right. There's no way we could have gone in a circle. It felt straight to me. We were hiking straight to the highway.

But there is the van, in plain sight. We were not walking straight. The knowledge crushes me. I feel pressed into the rocks. I did not get help for Dad and Gavin. I've wasted all this time.

My gaze stays on the van. It's too far to make anyone out. I don't see Gavin's slight form walking around. An intense fear stabs at my gut.

"Come on, let's get down there." I step off the ledge, trying to focus on where to put my feet. Loose rock and gravel shift and slide away under my shoes. I'm barely able to control my descent.

My head spins. Cooper would have been better off trying to get to the highway on his own. He says nothing as we descend. He just follows me and sometimes even helps steady my elbow as I stagger. I'm so grateful that Cooper is here to help.

"I guess I didn't hold up my end of the deal," I say, defeated.

"Yeah, well, we're not done yet. We can renegotiate the money later." Cooper smiles. It's a friendship smile, and this new feeling of belonging keeps me moving.

We're almost at the tree line, about halfway down the mountain. Stark is perched in a lodgepole pine, preening her feathers. When the rocks roll under my feet, she lifts her head and blinks down at me but makes no move to come. The sky behind her is filled with slate clouds.

The only thing I care about is getting back to the van. What are they doing right now? Are they even still there? I wonder if they think I've died or gotten lost. Maybe Gavin decided to go get help. Or maybe someone came along. My heart speeds up at this thought. Yes, maybe they're both safe. Dad could be recovering in a hospital right now. How wonderful would that be?

As I picture this, I become aware of the awful tension this responsibility has created in me. It's almost too heavy to bear any longer. Imagining Dad and Gavin safe floods me with sweet relief. But then wicked thoughts convince me that this is probably not what happened.

What am I going to do when I get to the van? I'll have to follow the road this time. Back to the highway in the direction we came from. About forty miles away. What was the last town we passed? I'd have to get to that gas station. Or maybe Free Hold is the closest place.

Cooper stops ahead of me, and I focus back to my surroundings. He's peering down, scratching his head. When I get closer, I see what he's looking at, and my heart shudders a little. It's another crevice in the rock. But this time it continues forever, stretching out on either side of us, separating us from where we need to go.

"Can you jump?" asks Cooper, turning to look at me.

I study the deep chasm across our path, craning my neck to see the bottom. It is much, much deeper than the one I fell in. The rock has split here, creating a fault line. There must have been an incredible noise when this happened—when years of freezing and thawing forced the rock to rip in two.

The span of it is wider in some places, but in this spot it looks as if I could lie across it and reach the other side—if I were a human bridge. The bottom is about six stories down. If Dead Skeleton Crevice had been half this deep, I would be dead along with Mr. Bones. Mr. Bones, who had a pocketful of money, but in the end, it didn't matter. He didn't have any friends to help him out.

Cooper is scanning behind us, and I know he's searching for another broken tree, but there isn't anything to use. As we look at each other, a stronger gust of cold wind hits me in the back, freezing my ears.

"Well, I guess I'll have to jump," I say.

"I'll go first," Cooper says as he cinches the straps on my pack he's carrying. "And then I can catch you."

Without any more warning or discussion, Cooper backs up a few steps before he charges. Throwing himself into the air, he hurtles across the chasm. I stop breathing, watching him sail over his certain death. He lands lightly on his feet. Turning to me, he grins, brushing his hands together as if that wasn't even a challenge.

"Easy," he says. "Now you."

I glance again at Stark, who is still perched on her branch. She stares straight ahead at nothing. I've watched her soar so many times. If only I could fly like her. I would have flown right out of here on that first day. Found the highway right off. When she flies, I follow her in my mind. But now I wish that she could really take me with her.

The wind picks up behind me and screams down the mountain like a charging rhino. It hits me in the back with icy fury. My body is alternating between sweating and freezing. With numb fingers, I pull my hoodie on and cinch the drawstrings.

"Come on! Hurry," Cooper calls to me.

I sneak closer to the rim and look across, trying to judge the distance. It's not too far.

"I can catch you," Cooper says, as if he can read my thoughts. "Trust me. I won't let you fall."

I shuffle my feet and look down again. A wave of dizziness sweeps over me, and I sway a little. I wipe the sweat that's trickling into my eyes. I've never felt so bone tired, so ill. A shiver clutches my muscles and holds tight.

Cooper makes an impatient sound. "Come on! I said I won't let you fall. You don't trust me? I came back for you, didn't I?" He throws his arms in the air. "Just believe in me, Karma."

My head snaps up. "What do you mean, *came back for me*?"

Cooper sucks in a breath and freezes. He closes his eyes and then nods as if he's decided something.

"I should have just told you. After I left you guys on the highway, I was good to go. I got another ride into town, found a bike. I was golden. But I . . . I couldn't stop thinking about your crappy van. I pictured you stuck on the side of that road with a flat tire and no one around to help."

A coldness creeps down my back that has nothing to do with the wind.

Cooper kicks a rock over the edge. It clips the side of the gorge with a little tick. I watch as it plummets. "I figured I'd just go check so I could stop wondering about it already. You weren't on the side of the road anywhere, and I was thinking *good, that's it then*.

"But then I saw your freaking bird. She's so white and hard to miss. It had to be yours. And then the stupid bike ran out of gas as I got to the end of the road. But you guys hadn't passed me. So I followed your bird, and when I found you, it was worse than I'd thought. I never saw your van in the ditch. I don't know why. I swear, Karma, I didn't know the tire would blow up!"

My voice comes out calmly, but inside I'm feeling like that exploding tire. "How did you know we'd have a flat tire, Cooper?"

He pauses.

"You were right when you said this is all my fault. It's always my fault. I screw up everything I touch." Cooper rubs a hand over his face. His shoulders are back to their usual slump.

I ask him again. "How did you know, Cooper?"

"I hated your perfect family. And then you dumped me on the side of the road just like everyone else in my life . . . so I slashed the tire."

The whole world fades away, and I feel as if I'm tilting off it. I picture him again on that day, his hair blowing through the window. He was at the back of the van near the tire. I picture his sharp knife we've been using this whole time.

Finally I point a shaking finger at him. "*Why?*"

I'm unable to find any more words. I can hardly see with the film of rage that has settled over me. All this time I've been traveling with Cooper, not knowing he's the one that caused our accident. I thought he was my friend. How could I have been so stupid? My hands clench, which brings a shooting pain that sears my left arm. My whole body feels hot and damp and sick. I collapse to my knees, holding myself up with one arm. I know I can't give up, but this betrayal has crushed the last bits of energy I have.

"Just leave me alone," I croak out. "Go away."

"Karma! Get up. You have to let me fix this. *I have to put your family back together!*" Cooper howls. His whole face turns red. Then he stops and takes a breath. "I'll do whatever you want," he says. "I'll leave you alone once we get help.

But right now, you have to get up and cross this before the snow comes."

I stare at him as something sharp and savage builds inside me. "You are not my friend."

Stark leaps then, and I glance up. She's flying above the trees, wheeling in slow, lazy circles. There's a cold front almost upon us, and my family is on the other side of those trees, waiting for me. What am I doing still on this mountain, crouching on the ground?

I climb to my feet and look around. The wind hits my face. I have to do this. Later I will hate Cooper. But right now I'm going to get to my family. I won't look at the traitor traveling with me.

I back up as Cooper did and then sprint to the edge. Just as I'm about to launch myself across the crevice, a hot wave of nausea grips me. I stumble at the last second. My leap is not enough to propel me to the other side. I reach for the edge.

And miss.

TWENTY-FIVE

I feel myself falling, but then Cooper's hand snakes out and snatches my wrist. It's my bad arm, and the pain of it nearly makes me pass out. I hang freely over the chasm. My vision is jerky and narrow, like looking through a camera lens. I see the rough rock in front of me, the open sky, and Cooper's wild eyes, which are green with flecks of light gold. There is impossible darkness below me. And Cooper's fingers dig into the red marks on my arm. He's on his stomach with his arms stretched out, clutching me. His face is strained.

"Don't let me go!"

"Climb," he grunts.

"Cooper, don't drop me. Don't."

He tries to pull me up, but he slips farther toward the edge. My right arm finally connects with the rock, and I grip it like a tree frog. The unbearable pressure on my injured arm lessens as my weight is transferred.

Our eyes meet. "Climb," Cooper says.

With Cooper pulling on my wrist, I claw with my other

hand, kicking my feet. The sharp edge of the rock rips the knees of my jeans as I teeter on the edge. The next moment, I'm scrambling over the rim.

Cooper and I lie on our backs, panting. We both take a moment to just breathe. But we have to keep moving or we're going to die up here.

When I try to stand, the ground spins around me. I stumble forward.

"What happened?" he asks.

"Nothing."

"You can hardly walk. Let me help you."

The last thing I want is to accept help from him, but we have to get off this mountain. I lean on Cooper's shoulder as he puts an arm around me.

"God, you're burning up," he says softly.

I know the direction I have to take. The image of the road and our van lying on its side is burned into my mind now. We lurch toward the forest. The only sounds I hear are the shuffling footsteps we make and my own heartbeat. Even the wind has stilled.

I search for Stark in the sky, knowing she'll love the coming snow. The first snow was always so exciting at home. It was a time for hunting. You can see tracks more easily. What I wouldn't give to be home now, getting ready for a hunt with Tank and Aunt Amy and Gavin. The fever is muddling my thinking. I can almost imagine that all of this was a dream and I'm going to wake up in my tree house and go clean the mews.

I stumble and come back to my actual circumstances.

150

I'm not hunting with Tank, I'm racing a clock. I'm racing toward our van that I left three days ago thinking I would be back in a few hours. With my head up, I keep marching, weaving in and out of balance. I need to stay upright. It's the only reason I allow Cooper to touch me.

"Karma, listen. These last few days—"

"Don't talk to me," I interrupt. My muscles ache with cold and stiffness.

Cooper remains quiet during the rest of our trek and keeps shooting me worried looks. His lips press together with fear. All his squawking and feather ruffling are absent now. There's no mask of indifference. I can read him plainly, but I don't care.

Finally I see things I recognize. The trees, those shrub bushes, and the shape of the boulders as we pass. We're on the road next, and I break from Cooper and wobble past the spot where I collapsed and called out for help a thousand years ago. Was it really just a few days ago? I feel as if I've aged a lifetime since then.

I fall down the steep embankment, sliding on my butt, holding my arm against me. "Gavin! Dad!"

And then I see him. Gavin in a woolen hat, his little white face shining like a moon peeking out of the van. The sight of him sends a jolt through me that travels straight to my heart.

I watch his expression shift from relief to dismay as he takes in my condition and the fact that there are no police cars or ambulances or doctors or firefighters behind me. There is only Cooper.

I give Gavin the short version of the last few days as we climb through the back doors of the van. Dad is under a blanket and still in the same place I left him.

"Dad, I'm here," I say. But he doesn't respond. He's so white, I can see little veins under his skin. I can't stand to see him helpless like this. This can't be Dad, my dad who always walks tall, always has a ready smile, and always crinkles up the corners of his eyes. Now he's small and pale and his beard is all messy and growing in. I don't know how Gavin has dealt with it all these days. "Dad, can you hear me?"

"He's been like that all day," Gavin says beside me. "He won't even drink anymore."

Gavin's face shows all the worry and fear he's had to live with by himself. It makes me want to scream and pound something. He's been stuck in this van, dealing with something no kid his age should have to deal with. The love I feel for my family overpowers me. I finally made it back to them. It almost doesn't feel real that Gavin is sitting in front of me alive and whole. Relieved, tears spill over and down my face. Gavin hugs me, then pats my shoulder as if I'm the younger one. I pull out the fortune game, dried hard and brittle.

Gavin takes it and stares at the paper glumly. "I didn't mean to give you a bad fortune. I don't want you to die."

"I know, Gav. I didn't, and we won't. We're all going to be fine. I'm making a new fortune. I'll be safe with my whole family at home very soon."

"I'm only making good fortunes from now on," he says.

I hear something and turn my attention to Dad.

"Dad! Are you awake? Please talk to me." I smooth his hair off his gaunt face and bend closer. My heart leaps as his head rolls away from me. His eyes open and he mumbles something, but he's not looking at me. I can see he isn't focused on anything.

He needs to get out of here, right now. All of us do.

Cooper. I can't believe I forgot about him. Where is he?

I lurch through the back doors and spy Cooper sitting on the ground next to the tipped-over van. His shoulders are shaking. My fever forgotten, I charge over to him but pull up when I see his face.

"It wasn't me. It wasn't me," he says, over and over. Cooper looks up at me, tears streaming down his face. He points to the perfectly whole right back tire that is in the air. The one that isn't shredded.

"That's the one I sliced."

When I first left the van in my desperate state, I hadn't even noticed which tire had blown out.

We lock eyes. The only things moving are the wet snowflakes beginning to fall around us.

"I have a do-over," Cooper says, his eyes pleading, searching my face for something I'm not quite ready to give.

I break our gaze and drop beside him, staring at the tires. "I guess we all get new futures. It's up to us to decide what to do with them."

TWENTY-SIX

Gavin was busy while I was gone. All the loose equipment that was tossed around in the accident is neatly back in place. He's swept out the broken glass and arranged everything neatly.

"Wow, you did a great job in here," I say, pulling out the first-aid kit. I need to get rid of this pounding in my head so I can think. Not wanting to use the last of our water, I crunch Advil and my antibiotics in my mouth. The bitter taste makes me scrunch up my face.

Gavin watches me with amusement and then casually points to a row of containers on the hawk box. My eyes widen. They're full of water.

"Where did you get this?" I ask.

"There's a creek behind the trees. Good thing I found it too; I drank all my water just after you left." He gives me a Gavin grin. "I had to make it livable in here. After the first night, we weren't sure where you were or how long it would take. At least we had the sleeping bags and stuff from the camping kit to stay warm."

They had water. All this time, that was my worst fear, and Gavin had solved it on his own.

Gavin's eyes go to a blackened fire pit just outside the door that I hadn't seen when I first rushed in. Only now do I notice the empty box by the door. Gavin's comic-book box. I know it's only comics, but my heart feels like it's breaking into a million pieces—with regret, and with pride at how Gavin has dealt with everything.

"Smart," Cooper says. He and Gavin appraise each other, and I wish I knew what they were both thinking. I give Gavin's shoulder a squeeze as I slump on a blanket he's laid out. I touch the cool water bottle to my forehead and close my eyes.

Every part of my journey, every bump and strain and scrape, sings on my body. I can't even think about walking the forty miles out on the road to the highway, but that's what I'm going to have to do. No messing around this time. Maybe if I had done that to begin with, we'd all be home by now. A desperate ache rolls over me.

I wish I could tie a message to Stark and have her fly out to wherever the people are. I haven't seen her since we were up on the mountain. But my worry for Dad trumps worrying about where she is. I'm so tired and worn down. If only someone else would come up with a plan. If only Dad were awake to tell me what to do. I sigh and open my eyes. I can't rest yet.

"How did you get here?" Gavin asks Cooper.

"Aha!" I yell, making Gavin and Cooper startle. "Gavin, you're a genius!"

"I am?" Gavin looks at me with confusion.

"Cooper's dirt bike." I'm sure I can learn to drive a dirt bike. It can't be any harder than anything I've done these past few days. I don't want to leave Dad and Gavin again. I want to bring them both with me, but it's impossible.

"It's out of gas," Cooper reminds me.

"We can take the gas out of our van and use it for the bike," I explain. "We had to do that once with our generator during a storm when our power went out."

"Huh?" Cooper says.

"Dad had to take gas out of the van because he'd forgotten to store gas for our backup generator. I watched him do it. I know I can do it again."

Cooper stares at me as if I've suddenly grown wings. "That's a good idea."

"It won't take me long to—" I begin.

Gavin interrupts. "Do you know how to drive a dirt bike, Karma?"

"Yes," I say.

At the same time Cooper announces, "*I'm* going."

We stare at each other, both with determined expressions.

"It's starting to snow, so driving a bike won't be easy," Cooper says. "And you're sick with a fever, and you have to use both arms to steer. It makes more sense for me to take the bike."

I know he's right, yet I don't want to have to depend on

him to actually come back. A small part of me remembers how Cooper helped me cross the chasm. How he saved me from the bear and wrapped me up on the mountain. But then I remember seeing him near our back tire when Dad let him off. I grab hold of the fury again.

"*I'm* going," I say.

"Do you want to waste time arguing about it, or should we get started?"

I give Cooper my most vicious stare. I am a newly caught accipiter, all wild eyed with sharp talons.

"My dad . . ." I begin, but then my throat stops me from saying more.

Cooper's gaze melts a little at the edges, but he says nothing. He turns and rifles through our stuff. Pulling out our black solar shower bag and hose system, he waves the hose at me and raises his eyebrows.

I shake my head. "That's too short. It won't reach the gas tank."

Then I remember what will work. I force myself up, still feeling sick and dizzy. I open our camping gear kit from under the bench seat and find our clear garden hose that we use to give water to the raptors.

"We'll use this," I say, holding it up. "And we can use that shower bag as a gas can, since it's heavy plastic. It's our portable camping shower. You can carry it to the bike."

We glance outside at the snow turning to rain, and I pull on my warm winter coat. My thoughts drift to Stark again, still out there somewhere. I face the open doors at the back and give a shrill whistle in case she's close but can't find us.

Maybe she's at the top of the mountain, where it's snowing. I turn away and focus on the task of getting the gas.

I immediately see that this will be a challenge because our van is sideways. The gas tank is up in the air. I can't climb up to put the hose down into the tank. This little obstacle makes me want to scream.

Cooper gently takes the hose from me and leads me to sit down. "This was a great idea, Karma. I've got it."

He vaults himself up onto the van. I can't help but be grateful he's here helping us.

"You have to feed the hose all the way down into the tank, 'til it touches the bottom," I advise from where I sit, watching.

"It won't fit."

"Cut the screw off from the end," I say. "Slice it at an angle so it's like a wedge."

"Are you sure you don't know how to do this from your secret life of crime?" Cooper flicks his knife out and cuts the hose before stuffing it into the gas tank, hand over hand.

"I'm surprised you don't know." Seeing the look on Cooper's face, I immediately wish I hadn't said that.

"Now what?" he asks. "There's no gas coming out."

"You have to bring the other end of the hose lower than the tank to allow gravity to take over."

Cooper drapes the hose off the side of the van and leaps down.

"Now you have to siphon it," I say. "You have to create suction in the hose, like a vacuum, to draw the gas out of the tank."

Cooper puts his mouth around the hose and sucks. After

a moment he gives up. "This is like trying to drink a thick milkshake."

"The gas has to travel the length of the hose, but once it gets started it'll come on its own. Keep trying. But be careful once the gas is close so you don't get it in your mouth."

Cooper tries again, taking breaks by kinking the hose to keep the suction in while he pants to get his breath. Finally I see the gas creeping along the hose toward us.

"Watch out, it's coming!" I yell.

Cooper jerks his mouth away from the hose just as gas bubbles out the end. He spits and gags as he stuffs the hose into the shower bag. "Yuck. It didn't get in my mouth, but the fumes are gross."

The bag bulges as it fills.

"You did it!" I can't help but cheer.

Cooper spits again. He hoists the heavy, awkward bag, and I can see him trying to figure out how he's going to carry it all the way to the berm where he left his bike.

"Carry it in here," I say, holding up my backpack. Cooper stuffs the gas into the pack and shoulders it.

"It's a couple hours' walk," I say, slipping my coat off. "You'd better wear this."

He takes my coat. "I'll be back as soon as I can, Karma. Just . . . trust me."

We share a look that screams loudly with all the things left unsaid.

My thoughts circle, going back in time. But the more I circle, the more confused I feel. Is it really all Cooper's fault? Is it mine? Is it anyone's?

Cooper's determined expression mirrors mine. One thing I know is that I need him now. And I think he needs us. If he's my friend, I have to trust him. With my father's life.

"Here's your do-over," I say.

Cooper nods once before stepping away. I watch him climb the slope until he disappears from view.

TWENTY-SEVEN

"He'll come back, right?" Gavin asks. I brush the hair out of his eyes and feel my heart swell with how smart he is. Even though he's only nine, he can sense something untrustworthy about Cooper. He can sense it, but I didn't at first. And I still don't want to.

"Sure he will," I say. And then we settle in under a sleeping bag for the wait.

Gavin shows me how he used emergency candles from the camping kit. "Dad suggested it," he says. He lights the stub of a candle perched on Stark's hawk box. "Even though it's a tiny flame, it cuts the frost and warms up the van 'cause it's a small space."

I peer out at the rain and the darkening sky. Stark is not coming back tonight. I slump against the side of the seat. But she stayed and hunted with me and kept me alive. That has to mean something. I can't help but feel she loves me.

"Stark saved me, Dad." I tuck the blanket under his chin.

He's deathly white, but I try to ignore that and keep fussing with putting extra blankets on him. I want to tell him all about what Stark did. He's not going to believe it. I'm bursting at the seams to let it all out.

The sun has set when we hear the faint sound of the dirt bike roar by on the road. Gavin and I stop what we're doing and stare at each other until the bike fades into the distance.

"Well, he got it running," Gavin says.

I nod. Cooper has a tank full of gas and a pocket full of money. He even has Dad's wallet. It was still in the pack. All Dad's credit cards. Cooper is set. What kind of friend will he be? What kind of friends are we now?

"Dad looks scared," Gavin says.

The candle flickers, creating weird shadows along the side of the van. Gavin and I each hold flashlights, and the pale light makes Dad's face look ghostly. The shadow of his beard blends with the darkness around him.

I pull Gavin down with me on the blanket behind Dad's seat. I give him half of my sleeping bag.

"Remember when Dad dressed up for Halloween with that black hat and a big hook on his hand?" I nudge Gavin in the arm teasingly. "And he waited in your room until you came in from chores? I could hear you scream across the whole house."

Gavin smiles and nods. "Yeah! That was funny." His eyes are brighter as he relives the memory. "Remember that time we went swimming at midnight?"

I can't help but grin at my favorite Dad memory. I was so shocked when he woke me up. Pressing a finger to his lips, he gestured at me to follow him to Gavin's room, then outside. It was so stinking hot that night, my pajamas stuck to me. We biked down to the pond, laughing at the novelty of being up so late. When we got there, we leaped into the water, making splashes that lit up under the light of the moon. Gavin and I used Dad's shoulders as a diving board over and over again. We swam in the cool, black water under the moonlight.

"Yeah," I say. "We should do that again next summer."

Gavin and I share our favorite memories of Dad to pass the time. It's a long, long night. No Stark. No Cooper. The temperature drops along with my hopes.

Will Cooper come back? A part of me knows he's not all bad inside. He was scared and fierce. When Stark nailed me, I didn't blame her; it's in her nature. Raptors are predictable as long as you stick to a routine and remember they are wild at heart. I know it's in Cooper's nature to fend only for himself, but I desperately hope that he won't leave us.

And that's when we hear it. The rumbling sound of vehicles approaching on the road.

Gavin and I stumble out the back doors. We're blinded by the floodlights aimed down at us from above. People spill down the slope, and voices call out.

Cooper skids toward me, and I'm about to hug him when I stop. I need to confess something.

"I didn't know if you were going to come back," I tell him. "I wasn't sure if I could trust you. I'm sorry, but I'm still mad at you for what you did."

Cooper pulls me into a hug. "Yeah, well, that makes two

of us." His touch grounds me, and it finally sinks in. We're rescued! They're going to take my dad to a hospital! I'm going to see Mom!

It's as if I'm finally able to share the burden of what's been resting heavy on my shoulders. My limbs begin to shake.

Through a strange slow-motion haze, I watch EMTs free Dad and put him on a stretcher. I can barely answer all the questions. I just nod and cling to Gavin and Cooper as we stumble up the hill after Dad.

It isn't until they've loaded Dad into an ambulance and we're about to climb in after him that I look up and search the sky. It's dark and cold, and there's no way Stark will fly to me, but I whistle and scream out her name.

"We have to go," one of the ambulance attendants says to me, clapping a hand on my shoulder.

I know what I have to do. I have to leave Stark behind.

When I finally climb in, the sound of the door slamming shut behind me cuts my soul in half.

TWENTY-EIGHT

We're sitting in the kitchen in our family meeting place. Mom is by the door, Dad is at the head of the table, and Aunt Amy leans against the counter with a cup of coffee in her hand. Gavin wiggles next to me. I look around at everyone in their usual places and have to squeeze my eyes shut to deal with the emotions. I'm so grateful to be home.

I can't stop glancing at Dad, as if seeing him healthy and whole is only a mirage. He's finally home from the hospital after almost a week. With his beard trimmed and his hair in a tidy braid, he looks like himself again, except for the cane leaning on his chair. My brother steals it and brandishes it like a sword.

"Dad needs that, Gavin," Mom says. "Remember what we told you about his circulation and blood clots?"

"That he needs his cane to help him move around?" Gavin returns the cane.

I ruffle his hair with my newly bandaged arm. I'm taking

my meds, but the doctors are worried there might be permanent damage. We're waiting to see, with strict orders not to overly exert myself or get my arm wet.

But we're all alive and together. We all made it back. Well, almost all of us made it back. As happy as I am, something inside of me is broken.

"Do you think Stark is still out there?" I ask Dad. "Near where the van went off the road?"

He sighs and rubs a hand across his beard. "I don't know, Karma," he says. "It's not very likely. You know that, right?"

I don't want to believe him. I abandoned Stark. We have to find her. I don't care anymore that she's supposed to go back to Canada. I just want to make sure she's safe and loved. I'd give anything to know she's alive.

"It's worth checking, though, right?" I ask.

"Going back to Free Hold is a tough decision right now, Karma," Mom explains. "You all need more time to recover."

Mom's probably right. But we've been recovering for a whole week. Besides, she's the one who looks the worst. Her skin is pale and her face has been pinched ever since she heard about my time in the crevice with Mr. Bones—who, we found out, was a missing hiker named Bill White. His family is happy to finally put his remains to rest.

"If Stark's out there, she'll come if I whistle," I say, not at all certain. "I know she will. We have to try."

"Trying may not be a bad idea," Aunt Amy says.

Mom and Dad look at each other, and something about it starts my heart racing.

"What? What's going on?" I ask.

"We know you need closure," Mom says, "but I have to go back to work, and Dad shouldn't be driving right now."

"But, please—" I beg.

"So we've hired some help," Dad says. "Someone who can help us with chores around here. And someone who can go with us to Free Hold to look for Stark. Today."

"What?" I leap up, and my stomach does a flip. "We're really going? And then . . . then if we find her, are we going to take Stark back to her owner?" I hate to bring it up, but I have to ask. I glance between Mom and Dad, trying to guess what they're thinking.

"That's quite a story of how you and Stark learned to hunt together," Mom says.

"That's my apprentice." Aunt Amy smiles at me.

"She's practically a member of the family now, isn't she," Dad says.

The hope rushes through me like a tsunami. "She saved my life," I say.

The fridge hums.

Finally I see the crinkles in the corners of Dad's eyes. "We feel that she's definitely earned her place here. And so does her owner. He said that if we can find her, after all you've been through, then she's yours."

"Ah!" I scream, grabbing my head on either side of my face. I'm going to cry.

"But, Karma." Dad looks me in the eyes until I stop bouncing. "I don't want you to get your hopes up. I really doubt we'll find her, but we'll certainly try."

167

I leap up and hug Dad, then go around the table and hug Mom. I grab Aunt Amy. "Thank you, thank you. We need to go right now. As soon as possible. I'm ready to go now."

"Can I stay here?" Gavin asks. "I need to spend some quality time with Spider-Man."

I chuckle. I wouldn't want to go back out there if I were him either.

"When are we leaving?" I ask. "Who is the new help?" My whole body itches to be on the road. I have to find her.

"Cooper should be here soon," Dad says.

"Cooper?" Everything grinds to a halt, and I stare at Dad. He stares back, looking quite pleased with himself. I'm speechless as I hear a vehicle pull up.

"That must be him," Dad says, winking at Mom. "Amy's apprentice Bret picked him up."

I don't even have time to sort out how I feel before Cooper walks into our kitchen, behind Mom.

"'Sup," Cooper says.

"'Sup yourself," I say.

Cooper looks different in a clean jacket and new cargo pants. Suddenly I realize that I've really only known him for a few days. He eyes me a little shyly, as if he's nervous too.

"What are you doing here?" I blurt out.

"How's your arm?" he asks at the same time.

Cooper gives a small grin. I feel us shifting back in sync.

"Karma," Dad says, "why don't you guys go pack Aunt Amy's truck for the trip?"

TWENTY-NINE

As I take Cooper through the mews, he tells me everything that's happened to him since we separated at the hospital. He had to confess to stealing the bike. It was hard, but he turned in the money he'd taken too.

When he called his father right after everything happened, his dad didn't even ask how he was, just wished him luck. It was his uncle Mike who came to claim him. I want to cover his hand with mine when he tells me that part.

"I have to pay restitution for the bike and the phone," he explains. "Your dad and your aunt worked it out with the police. I can work off my offenses by volunteering here. Cutting up tidbits for birds, or something like that."

I take out a quail and place it on the cutting board. "You can start learning right now," I say. "We've got to bring Stark's lure."

Cooper pulls the knife out from his pocket. The metal clip glints along the black handle. His fingers flick it open, and we peer at each other over the blade that started it all.

Or at least it could have.

Cheeko chooses that moment to cast a long pellet. Cooper's mouth drops open in disgust, which makes me laugh. He slices the quail in half lengthwise, like a natural.

"Karma," Aunt Amy yells from the house. "Ready? Your dad's in the truck."

I grab what we need, toss it into a satchel, and race Cooper to the truck.

"Stark will come," he says to me after we climb in. "She's your bird."

"She isn't mine. No one really owns a falcon," I say. "If they trust us and respect us enough, they allow us to be their partners."

As we turn around in the driveway, I can see the training area where I thought I had flown Stark for the last time.

"Did I tell you," I say to Cooper, "that in medieval times, gyrfalcons were only flown by royalty?"

"My lady," Cooper says, with a low bow from his seat, "Thou hast graced me with your lovely presence and weird, bossy nature."

I laugh.

"And getting weirder every day," I say. "I will allow you to scrub the mews later, as my royal page."

Dad gives me a sideways look.

Being weird is much better when there's someone to be weird with.

As we drive toward Free Hold, it feels right to have Cooper by my side. This land is somehow ours. We know it too well. Rolling hills, baked brown and dotted with sagebrush. A pronghorn watches us go by. The sun hangs cheerily above the ever-present mountain range in the distance.

When we make our stop, the four of us stand on the road, shielding our eyes.

I pull on my gauntlet and picture Stark soaring high, far from here.

She could be anywhere. What would make her stay in this area? Even though she's an imprint, and trained to a lure, being in the wild this long might've awakened all her instincts by now. She learned to hunt. She can survive out here without me. Right?

Aunt Amy hands me the lure. Cooper unlatches Stark's empty box and looks to the sky. Dad leans into his cane and gives me a nod.

I take a deep breath and swing the lure high. I whistle with everything I have, hoping that all my love for Stark will flow out of me and she'll hear and know it. The lure keeps swinging as I search the sky.

Please choose me, Stark. Please.

And then a shadow passes over.

AUTHOR'S NOTE

Falcon Wild is a story in keeping with what I love to write about—gritty outdoor adventure and the realistic portrayal of the special relationships humans can form with animals.

I do not have years of personal experience as a falconer. What I do have is an intense fascination with the sport of falconry and the people who devote their lives to it. Falconry isn't just a sport, but a lifestyle. It requires incredible amounts of time, resources, and patience. It's also uncommonly rewarding—allowing humans to work closely with an animal and forge a bond.

I admire the men and women who choose to follow their passion, and I'm grateful for the support and assistance of those who answered this newbie's naive questions.

The challenge of writing *Falcon Wild* was to stay true to the details of modern-day falconry, while crafting satisfying storylines and characters. In creating this story, I chose to alter common practices for effect in a few scenes.

For example, in the first chapter Stark bites Karma after

her hood comes off. Normally this only happens in the context of food. If a falconer is taking food away, a poorly trained falcon may bite.

Additionally, in the story Stark's owner does not contact Karma's family for months after she goes missing. In reality, falconers are normally vigilant about where their birds are. A missing raptor picked up by another falconer can often be sorted out quickly through the identification band that all raptors carry. Of course there are exceptions, as displayed in my fictional story.

Lastly, the hunting scenes with Stark may give the impression that it is relatively easy for a raptor to take down game. But it takes practice for this kind of partnership to work. And in real life, a successful hunt is not measured in game taken but by how well the raptor flew.

For more information, I suggest the following websites:

International Association of Falconry and Conservation
    of Birds of Prey
    http://www.iaf.org/index.php

The Modern Apprentice
    http://www.themodernapprentice.com/index.htm

North American Falconers Association
    http://www.n-a-f-a.com

Ontario Hawking Club
    http://www.ontariohawkingclub.org

ACKNOWLEDGMENTS

Thank you to my dear critique partners, Amy Fellner Dominy, Marcia Wells, and Sylvia Musgrove, for eagle-eyed, multiple readings. And to my early readers, Helen Landalf, Tess Hilmo, Kristin Lenz, Sara Bennett Wealer, and particularly Kathy McCullough, who kept me on track each Sunday. Thank you to Jackie White for being there to read every single thing I write. And to Jody Kyburz, Olivia Countryman, and Madison Countryman for taking the time to provide feedback.

Special thanks go to my technical advisers, who patiently answered questions and tried to explain the finer nuances of falconry: Gary Selinger, falconer; Matt Lieberknecht, master falconer; and Maya Basdeo, falconer and conservation and outreach liaison with the Ontario Hawking Club. I'm so grateful to these kind people who helped me infuse my story with accuracy and authenticity. (Matt even let me fly his gyr.) Any errors in this story are mine alone.